The Osprey's View

D1121214

The Osprey's View

Lucia Peel Powe

The Osprey's View

Cover and Interior design by Ted Ruybal
Manufactured in the United States of America

For more information, please contact:

Wisdom House Books
www.wisdomhousebooks.com

Paperback ISBN 13: 978-0-692-56194-2
FIC000000—FICTION / General
LCCN: 2015957935
1 2 3 4 5 6 7 8 9 10

The cover artwork was done by:
Francis Speight (1896-1989) Sans Souci Ferry, Spring
Courtesy of the NC Museum of Art

Additional illustrations by
Vita Jones, Myra Bowen, Emily Eve Weinstein, Pamela Henry Pate
Christine Amory Long & Elaine O'Neil.

A portion of the proceeds from the sale of this book will go to the
Roanoke River Partners
www.roanokeriverpartners.org

The Osprey's View

is dedicated with love to:

Judge Elbert Sidney Peel, Jr.,
who introduced me to his beloved Roanoke River;

and to our children:
Lucia Claire Peel,
Sarah Margaret "Mimi" Peel Roughton,
Lily Peel Elkins, her daughter;
Sydney Eldridge Peel Woodside,
Joseph "Woody" Woodside, her husband,
Stewart Woodside, their daughter,
Joseph "Joey" Woodside, their son;
Elizabeth Chase Peel,
David Solow, her husband, and
Ruby Marlette Solow, their daughter.

Table of Contents

Acknowledgments

Gratitude to

Clara Jackson and Ted Ruybal of
Wisdom House Books

•

Editor Linda Whitney Hobson

•

Artists:
Vita Jones
Myra Bowen
Emily Eve Weinstein
Pamela Henry Pate
Christine Amory Long
&
Elaine O'Neil

Introduction of
Lucia P. Powe's first book

Roanoke Rock Muddle

(2003)

by Doug Marlette
(1949-2007)

When I taught a course in Humor Writing at the UNC School of Journalism and Mass Communication, the Dean told me we had to restrict classes to UNC journalism students: no creative-writing students or drama students. Soon, even among the journalism pool, this course was overloaded with applicants—we had room for thirty but twice that on the waiting list.

About that time, I got a call at home from Lucia Powe asking if she could take my class. I said I'd be delighted to have her in my class, but she'd have to take it up with the Dean. So she did. Guess who

won. On the first night of class, Lucia was there, but how did that happen?

I know how: She was persistent. She was insistent. She would not take "No" for an answer. She would not be discouraged. And those are the qualities of artists. And that's how she wrote this novel.

I love *Roanoke Rock Muddle* because it is so much like Lucia herself: it teems with life. I love her characters, too, for being fabulous and formidable in the best ways possible. Reading this book, I could walk the streets of Williamston, North Carolina, navigate tides the color of hoecake batter on the river barge Swamp Monkey, see and smell the Roanoke River and the Albemarle Sound, and taste the oyster pie and Rock Fish Muddle. I could smell the bacon and fatback frying and hear the streak o'lean sizzling in Ben Olive's kitchen.

The book is full of fond memory, keen observation, delightful detail, vivid characters, colorful language, and the hardest and rarest of things to accomplish in a novel: it is full of surprises. Writing is hard work. Certainly the hardest thing I've

ever done was writing a novel. Everything conspires against the writing of a novel. One should not do it unless one has to. It is lonely work. Your only ally and cheerleader is yourself. You must care. I am grateful that Lucia cared because now the State of North Carolina, the world and I am richer for it. I know Lucia even better than I did before I read *Roanoke Rock Muddle.*

Reynolds Price writes that there's no such thing as a young novelist, suggesting that all novels are about time, the passage of it, and what we learn from marinating in its passage. The novelist's tools are memory and experience deeply registered. Lucia's novel is a perfect example of what he was talking about, a product of that mysterious alchemy as only she can conjure it.

Lucia Powe may have been officially designated one of my students in Humor Writing, but I'm sure I learned more from her than she did from me. Definitely one of my favorite students, she was serious about funny and brought great energy to learning about writing funny. Even so, the truth was: she

did not need the class! She was already funny, thus there was nothing I could teach her. Lucia is a natural humorist, with an ear and an eye for the comic detail, yet she never went for the cheap laugh and remained a Southern lady throughout. She didn't descend below her raising, and she still wrote funny, holding her own without abandoning her principles.

Most importantly, in all of her class papers, Lucia had a voice. And that voice was straight out of eastern North Carolina. Others in the class were trying to fabricate a voice, but Lucia's came to her naturally, imbuing her stories with authenticity, sensitivity, humility, and hard-won wisdom.

As we all know, Lucia Powe is beautiful as well as talented, which can be as much a burden as a gift for those who possess it. People tend to focus on your surface and resent or underestimate you. After reading *Roanoke Rock Muddle* I can report, for the tiny fraction who didn't know, that Lucia is as beautiful inside as she is outside. And, adding to the energy of her work, her inner beauty comes through loud and clear in her writing.

Doug Marlette (1949-2007), a Pulitzer Prize-winning editorial cartoonist and the author of *Kudzu*, the long-running comic strip, and *Kudzu: A Southern Musical*; as well as *Shred This Book: The Scandalous Cartoons of Doug Marlette* (1988); and two novels, *The Bridge* (2001) and *Magic Time: A Novel* (2007), was a friend of Lucia Peel Powe, introducing on October 2, 2003, her first novel, *Roanoke Rock Muddle* (2003), to the readers of Chapel Hill, N.C.

Preface

The Osprey's View

Spring 1941

ten-foot wooden motorboat swerved around, negotiating with difficulty the rapidly-racing current of the Roanoke River, when the shortest of three men crowded in lost his footing and, thereby, control of his tiller. The second man was flung into the bottom of the boat, and the third man, the tallest, was thrown backward, slamming into the gunwale before sliding broken-backed into the swift, cold water.

How in hell did this happen? Did the boat crash into a submerged rock? Did it collide with an underwater cypress stump?

Sixteen seconds earlier, perched atop the tallest cypress in the Conine Swamp beside the Roanoke, the deepest and swiftest river on the Eastern Seaboard, a two-year-old mother osprey spied a weather-beaten motorboat buzzing south directly toward her. Far, far below her perch, the tea-colored waters of the majestic swamp oozed out into the river's battercake-colored waters. This ancient river carried melted snow from the mountains of Virginia and valuable topsoil from the farmlands of Virginia and North Carolina down to and through the Albemarle Sound on its way to the Atlantic Ocean. In spring, the swift current pulled even the normally stagnant waters around the tannin-soaked roots of the swamp's lacy cypress trees into its race to the sea.

An area of the bird's brain might have concerned itself with her two nestlings only twenty feet away, alone in their nest on top of a less-tall cypress. However, at this moment her eyes were focused on a small boat overloaded with three men fishing as they puttered down-river near the swampy shoreline. She may not have recognized the men as

humans, or even cared what they were. However, she did recognize their catch—fresh, live fish collected in a large bucket as the perfect lunch for her two babies.

She streaked down, looking neither left nor right, and snatched a lively striped bass from the rusty fishing bucket, then soared up to her nest with the fish wriggling in her talons. The osprey turned the fish in her talons after she was in the air so that it faced forward, like a skater's blade under her. Quite pawky for so young a bird, yes? Well, all hell had broken loose in the boat below.

The moment she lit on the bucket, but before she flew away with her catch, in that quick second, all three jumped up startled from their seats and almost flipped the boat. When they realized that one of them *had* been thrown into the water, the two remaining men howled with laughter, struggled with the motor, and turned the boat in the direction of their mate.

But the boat was having trouble reaching their friend in the spring-swollen river. He was swept

out to deep and swifter middle-river, then fast away downstream. The small craft sputtered along after, its motor not designed for speed. And the third man, the poor fella in the water, seemed not to be helping them by swimming in their direction. In fact, he seemed not to be swimming at all.

Truth was, he was barely keeping his head above water in this mad spring river rushing hell-bent to the ocean.

So simple. All so simple. An innocent swamp beauty, the osprey, hunting for then gathering a perfect meal. The sun kept shining and a pileated woodpecker in his formal tuxedo suit kept hammering at an ancient cypress trunk, both bird and tree well at home in the wide, antediluvian swamp.

From the west bank across the river a black bear, too, had been fishing—slapping for fish in the shallows to feed her two cubs. Her right paw hesitated in mid-air as she noted the curious activity across the river. Then she returned to her maternal duties on this good day for fishing.

Chapter One

Four Views of a Wedding

St. James Episcopal Church,
West Franklin Street, Richmond, Virginia

—June 1940—

*I*n the moments before the Whittington-
Haughton wedding began, historic St. James
Episcopal Church was filled with the reso-
nant sounds of organ, violin, cello and bass playing
Bach's "Jesu, Joy of Man's Desiring."

∼ View One ∼
The Groom's Former Girlfriend
Elizabeth Ann Shannon (Betty Ann)

How I do hate and despise that rich, black-haired woman down there in her grandmother's old droopy lace dress. Neither she nor her mother seems aware of the current styles. And neither has ever, apparently, tweezed her eyebrows. Almost every woman these days plucks, shapes, tweezes her eyebrows to a fine skinny-shaped line. Sometimes they are shaped to lift high above their eyes in a permanent look of surprise, interest or disdain. Sometimes, they are 'penciled' in, as most of their real brows have vanished.

Where the devil did I go wrong? Or was I always wrong . . . in thinking that Chase and I were . . . meant for each other. For me, anyway, that thought went nowhere. Not meant for each other. And to think, those four years in Raleigh at St. Mary's . . . I dated dozens of boys at State, Carolina and Duke. But all casually, assuming that I was the intended of . . . that

boy-down-there-at-the-altar-with-that-rich-woman-with-the-eyebrows!

I thought . . . I knew that when he finally . . . finally, finished med school and came back home . . . we would marry, of course, and spend a happy, normal life together. I even completed the secretarial course at St. Mary's, and I hate being a secretary, so I could help in Daddy's law office until our babies came. I had the puzzle pieces so neatly fitted together, orderly, fused. What in God's name . . . went . . . wrong?

Oh, my God. Chase was also my chief marshal at the state debutante ball. He seemed so proud when I was invited to be an assistant leader.

Lord, I've had this crazy swooning crush on him since kindergarten. I spent years trying to hide it, to show a calm, cool attitude . . . so he wouldn't feel . . . crowded. Did he not feel **anything**? He was always sweet, fairly attentive, listened to me when I talked to him . . . Never rude . . . Never crude. But he treated everyone that way, so that was also a part of this betrayal—his kindness.

Kind, just like his father, Doc Haughton. How

much of his behavior was merely good manners, his Mama's rearing, and how much was an interest in me? Was any of his attentiveness to me . . . because he liked, maybe loved me . . . special? Or was I always just . . . a nice girl in the crowd?

*Have I painted myself into a corner? No more young single men exist in all of Martin County. All the boys in eastern Carolina are already married. I'm twenty-five years old! Been typing for Daddy as his legal secretary, I guess, for five years! Now, I must not cry. I must think how **that** would look!*

The pew began shaking slightly—like the very early signs of an earthquake—as Betty Ann strove to control herself.

*What will **happen** to me? There are no men, **anywhere**, not my age. There's that single dentist, but he's twenty years older than I am. Well, I'll just have to do the ladylike thing, the Christian thing, forgive Chase first, for what? He never proposed to me. He never asked me to "go steady." He never promised me anything. He's broken no promises, offered no ring, no fraternity pin.*

*I am as crazy as a loon. What was I **thinking** all these years? How could I be so **dumb**, so **blind**? I can't even discuss it with Mama, not with anybody. Nobody. But . . . if that girl had not married him . . . I believe . . . I am convinced . . . absolutely positively that . . . we would have . . . married. I know it.*

So . . . here . . . here and now, I will do the only thing I can. Only thing left for me to do. I shall become that woman's best friend. I shall be Saravette Whittington's . . . very . . . best . . . friend.

⤳ **View Two** ᵔ
The Bride's Former Boyfriend
Richard "Bass" Baskerville

—ᴍ—

What in hell am I doing sitting back here with my family when I should be down there marrying that girl? All my life I knew, and my family, too, that she would marry me. From first grade up, she was my girlfriend, my tennis partner. I don't know if I was actually in love with Saravette. How does a guy fall in love with a girl . . . who seems to try to put him off in a way, although sweetly, all the time. A girl who is smarter than he is, beats him at tennis most times, who seems so satisfied without him or any boyfriend. No necking, smooching, or smacky-mouth for her! She needed no one else. She never needed to be a couple. I must have dated every girl I wanted to in a hundred-mile radius and slept with many, but when I turned to Saravette, I hardly knew where to start. I still thought we'd make it, even when she went off to Julliard. I never believed she'd go all the way with that concert pianist business. And see here? She didn't!

My family never said anything directly, but I've often caught them looking at me in surprise, confused, as if ready to question me, "Hey, what happened?" or more like, "What didn't happen?" They knew that, with their blessings, I had taken her on numerous house parties, well-chaperoned, of course, to our house in the mountains for skiing. Everyone accepted us as an 'item' . . . though nothing much was going on between us. She did not mind when I dated other girls and vice-versa. But still, I had assumed . . . .

He looked at the bride's mother, Genevieve, in the front pew, and back at Saravette in front of Father Simpson, who was going on.

Neither of them wears much make-up at all. Don't need to and, anyways, both of them are out-door women. Genevieve, an elegant woman, likes the image of herself on horseback, I think. Saravette plays tennis with her daddy on Saturdays and takes tennis lessons when she isn't at the piano.

Bass had always been impressed by the emphatic resemblance between the two women: their dramatic black eyebrows.

There are portraits at the Whittington house, painted when the women turned twenty. They looked almost identical, with the familiar heavy eyebrows, except for Saravette's pretty little mole. I'm going to miss that girl—damn her pretty hide!

~ View Three ~
The Bride
Saravette Whittington

Saravette Whittington was, for 1940, a mature bride of twenty-four with intelligent brown eyes, a perfect tiny mole on her left cheek and naturally wavy brunette hair from her mother's family. She stood patiently in the church vestibule through "Jesu, Joy of Man's Desiring," poised between her father and her maid of honor at crusty, beautiful St. James Episcopal Church. "Crusty" because it served the "upper crust" of old Richmond.

The church prided itself, too, on serving other levels of the Richmond citizenry and attempted quite serious outreach programs for the needy. It also served the girls at venerable St. Catherine's prep school across the street and St. Christopher's prep school for boys a few blocks away and had the best darn church choir in town, offering up somewhat "high" church music, strong on Buxtehude, Bach, Handel and Haydn.

Saravette loved the old story about Bach and thought of it even now as she listened to his beloved music. She sniffed at the large calla lily in her wedding bouquet as she pictured the young Johann Sebastian Bach walking two hundred miles to meet, visit, and, he hoped, study with Buxtehude. He stayed with his teacher for several years.

This striking though not blushing bride listening to the music she had chosen was careful to stand out of the way of late-arriving guests. Saravette tried not to check again the uneven hemline of her grandmother's gown. The seamstress had tried her heart out to make it even, but it had hung in the attic wrapped in bed sheets for too many years to hang evenly today.

Her maid of honor, Estelle Watkins, wearing soft mauve chiffon and carrying dyed roses of the same color, was standing supportively to one side. Saravette's dear favorite tennis partner, her father, Gavin Whittington, was at her other elbow. A calm bride, Saravette gently shushed the harried wedding director, or mistress of ceremony, who busily spread

her nervous jitters everywhere she lit, though wearing her most appropriate and calming long navy-blue gown with a single strand of pearls. Stern and proper, except for her jaunty little navy velvet cocktail hat with the feather that danced over her left eye, she was very much the mode.

Saravette had been allowed to choose every selection of music, though very little else for that year's most outstanding social event, the Haughton-Whittington wedding. Normally, Dr. Hooten, the organist, might suggest the music, or the bride's mother. Not this mother.

This mother, the formidable and still beautiful Genevieve Whittington, was tone-deaf and so allowed, no, insisted her equally beautiful daughter select her own music, just as she had required her to study piano from the moment the little four-year-old had been seen picking out songs such as "Three Blind Mice" and "Frère Jacques" on the family instrument that no one else had played for thirty years.

Mrs. Whittington's maid, Violet, told everyone that she saw the whole thing and that, "Miz' Genevieve

clasped her hands and looked straight up to heav'n and said right out loud, 'Dear God, I know you are telling me to raise up this child in the way she should go. You are surely showing me that you've given her this gift, as no one else in the family has ever had it, and it's up to me and her father to allow this talent to blossom . . . to make it bloom and flower.' That's exactly what she said to her God. I was standing right out in the hall and heard and saw it all." True, but Violet was inclined to stretch a story sometimes.

"Little Miss Music" began kindergarten the next year at St. Catherine's School and would have attended all twelve years there except she graduated from high school a year early, having been accepted at Julliard music conservatory to major in piano.

Very few Richmond girls of Saravette's age were urged to advance in the arts at that time. Not that these young ladies had no talent, but their parents preferred to promote "social" arts: a degree, or at least two years at an appropriate college and experience in decorating, entertaining, raising funds for select charities and Junior League activities. The

idea, no need to explain, was that this would lead to a husband, ideally a professional, who could support this lifestyle and their offspring's attendance at the same select schools. Every quarter-century or so, they hoped to repeat the same events to everyone's satisfaction, particularly the grandmother's.

Who could dislike such a simple recipe as this?

Saravette's father, Gavin, an investment banker, took care of the other required area: tennis! He wanted all bases covered with this, his only child of whom so much was expected. He trained little Saravette in tennis just as strenuously as her mother force-fed piano. The little girl's sense of timing and quick reflexes seemed to count for good in both directions.

Mother Genevieve could hardly believe that such a talent had been born unto her and now thought like her, mostly. Tho' Genevieve was tone deaf, she nonetheless listened to her baby's every little sonatina with rapt dreaminess. Daddy Gavin was mostly supportive of the music, except when it interferred with their tennis. However, he was once heard to

say, "If I hear 'Country Gardens' one more time, I'm going to drink acid."

Saravette had gamely fulfilled her parents' hopes for her, but today's wedding was not the culmination of her parents' plans.

Now she turned to the nervous wedding director, reassuring her that everything was perfectly under control. Then she smiled to herself, wishing she could see, touch and smell sweet Chase, back there in the choir's dressing room, waiting with his father, Doctor Haughton, to join her and her father at the altar. She turned to her father as he shifted from one foot to another.

Gavin mused, *Am I prepared to walk this baby, my only daughter, down the long aisle to that young man, give her to him to be carried away . . . I assume forever. Hell no!* His stomach hurt. He wanted to cry, but he knew his girls, Genevieve and Saravette, would never forgive him. His earlier Scotch "quickie," offered by one of the eight groomsmen, was not helping.

Saravette winked at him, clutched his arm,

leaned up and kissed him on the cheek to calm him. He really was her favorite man in the world, except now Chase was right up there with him. If her mother had lavished her with the best music teachers money could buy, her father had done equally well with tennis instructors. He began hitting balls with her when she was five and escorting her from age nine on up to the best tennis courts in Virginia.

She remembered her parents disagreeing over her summers at music camp or tennis camp. Gavin had won that one. Because Gavin had no sons, tennis was the one sport he and she could share. She remembered tennis lessons every Saturday morning. She played with her father at least once a week, usually on Sunday afternoon, and with her country club youth team on Wednesday afternoon. All this was interspersed with attending and playing in tournaments that her parents attended religiously. She could sometimes outplay her father, but she always outplayed her mother.

Keyboard instruction was scheduled every Monday and Thursday afternoon at 4:00. She practiced a

minimum of two hours a day after third grade, sometimes more. Schoolwork came easily to her, because she had learned to read before starting school and never stopped. She was not prone to giggle and chitchat during study hall, but tried to race through as much homework as possible because there was so little time the rest of the day. She considered her study hall time a special gift, not to be wasted. Fortunately for busy St. Catherine's girls, there were no boys on the premises with whom to flirt.

Saravette remembered, however, how St. Catherine's girls looked forward to seeing St. Christopher's boys at parties and on weekends at dances organized for the two schools, sometimes referred to as brother-sister schools. And, ah, yes, later on during high school, weekends were arranged with other Virginia all-male prep schools: Virginia Episcopal School in Roanoke, Episcopal High School in Alexandria, that the alumni modestly referred to as "the" high school, and Woodberry Forest School—out in the middle of nowhere.

Saravette wished she could have known Chase

when he was playing football at Episcopal High, but he was several years older. And besides, he might not have liked her then. He attended Davidson College, near Charlotte, North Carolina, after prep school. Davidson was a small, highly respected Presbyterian men's school that regularly pumped out future lawyers, doctors and even a couple of U.S. presidents. She could not have met him then anyway, because for much of the time she was pounding away at the keyboard at Julliard in New York City.

Saravette had very little social life, but, oh, was she happy there! Largely because she knew what she was doing and did it well. No doubt, too, because she received piles of praise, and healthy criticism, not only from the faculty, but also from her fellow students. They were not envious but proud to be her classmate. They all wanted to share her spotlight on short student tours and with area symphony orchestras.

Here today, however, instead of bowing to appreciative audiences who were entranced by her rendition of Beethoven's Fifth, our queen for the day, the happy smiling bride, was grimacing with

pain in the vestibule of St. James Church, preparing to give it all away, her promising music career. Give it up for a country doctor from coastal North Carolina. This pain came not from that decision, though, but from her blistered heels: her new, not "broken-in" ivory-dyed silk wedding pumps were rubbing massive blisters. She imagined limping down the aisle, leaning on her father for support, tears of pain streaming down her face for all to see and wonder at. She leaned down to remove her shoes when the most competent wedding planner in all of Richmond rushed over.

"Dear, dear, no. Your pretty little feet have surely swollen with all the standing, but you won't be able to get them back on! No, no, no. Please keep your shoes on!"

Helplessly, hopelessly, Saravette gazed soulfully into her eyes. "Miz' Harper, had we rather I walk down the aisle with burst, broken, bloody blisters on my heels or go down barefoot?" She tried to smile as she said it to soften the blow. Poor Miz' Harper had no answer and was all the more miserable.

"Why do I *do* this?" she mumbled, near tears.

Bach's "Jesu, Joy of Man's Desiring" was finally winding down, the bride noted and, after this, she should have the fourth course of a musical lunch, Bach's "Sheep May Safely Graze," during which her mother would be escorted to her pew. Saravette had originally requested an all-Bach wedding, but Dr. Hooten had talked her out of it. "Just too, too, too, way too formal," he insisted.

Ah well, she thought, *maybe next time . . . silly thought. What next time? Speaking of silly, I've been told more no's in the last six months than I've ever heard in my whole life put together. Is that a good omen?*

"How can you be so calm, so relaxed?" begged Estelle, still beside her, but antsy. "Oh, of course, it's all those recitals. Naturally, you're not nervous, you're not self-conscious in front of crowds," she whispered. "But marriage, it's so final!" she grieved.

"Oh, darn, Saravette . . . your earring, your new pearl earring!"

Saravette, flowers in her left hand, reached for her right ear. Her pearl earring was gone. Now

she panicked. Her father jumped back. The whole group danced around, looking on the floor, under feet, under long-swinging tulle and chiffon skirts. Crawl, search, crawl, search.

Now, only now, her magical calm imploded. "They're the pearls Chase gave me as a wedding gift!" she wailed, as softly as one can wail. She grabbed for her pearl necklace. It was safe. She explained to no one in particular, "Daddy and Mother gave me the necklace and Chase the earrings. I can't get married without my pearls!" Finally, giving up, she removed the other pearl button and slipped it into her father's pocket.

"Honey," her daddy patted her hand, "Insurance will take care of it. Don't worry. It can be replaced."

"No, Daddy. Chase has no insurance. He hasn't started working yet." She was heart-broken, but the "Wedding March" was soon to tune up after her mother was seated and she stood up tall, pressed her bouquet to her middle and took a deep breath, hoping no one would notice her bare, stockinged feet under her grandmother's wedding dress and her naked ear lobes.

Estelle squeezed her arm. "I'm so sorry. But still

. . . how are you so calm?"

Saravette, taking her father's arm, pressing his wrist to assure him, looked quietly, confidently at her childhood best friend and then up at her tennis partner.

"Because . . . I know exactly what I'm doing."

─◦ **View Four** ◦─

The Mother of the Bride
Genevieve Whittington

─◦◦◦─

That child has no idea what she's doing. She has no notion of what marriage involves. She appears wise and intelligent, but she is one of the most naïve females I've ever known. My fault, no doubt. Her father is quite right. I have never told her anything about anything . . . of consequence. How could I? No one ever told me anything, either. I trusted the Physical Education Department at St. Catherine's to tend to all that. Why do we send them there if they can't, won't, handle those duties, those technicalities . . . preparing girls for womanhood?

What is a 'prep school' for, for mercy's sake, if they don't prepare them for one of their major duties and responsibilities? My baby leaves soon for Martin County, North Carolina. She thinks it will be heaven . . . a small village where everyone knows everyone else by their first name. She tells me they help one another during spring

planting, when anyone is sick or dies. The churches are full every Sunday. Nirvana.

Of course, I can see why she's enchanted by this boy, his family and his wonderful town. I was selfish in hoping she'd marry one of the boys here, in Richmond, partly to be near us, because we would already know his family and she could continue her career . . . of course. She might teach at the college, have a manager organize her concert tours from Richmond . . . maybe not to Europe.

But maybe yes to Europe, why not? Her teachers say she is capable enough to tour anywhere and, being so . . . like our family, she can handle it. If she had babies, we could help, with nurses to keep them while she toured. Now, Genevieve, are you trying to live another life through that girl? . . . And you don't want her to disturb your dreams for her? Daddy says I've got to let go. Let her loose. Got to let her go.

I reminded him that here in Richmond she is known and accepted, more than accepted, admired, well, envied . . . If I do say so myself, and I think her father agrees, we've done an admirable job rearing

that special girl. Spoiled her, perhaps. But no, she couldn't be spoiled. She never asked for anything. Maybe because we had already given her everything . . . hmmm. She never even asked for a car . . . even when several of her friends had received cars. It never occurred to her that she needed an automobile.

But now, giving up her music! After those years at Julliard! Giving up on her dreams. My dreams? Her concert tours. Throwing away her established situation here to move to a village, a country tobacco town of a few thousand souls. What will she do with her music? Her tennis? Who will be her friends? Chase is a Presbyterian. Will she be comfortable in his church?

Do the women play bridge? Saravette does not. Do they all cook for their husbands? She has no notion. Never read a cook book. Never lifted a frying pan. St. Catherine's does not offer home economics. Nor did Julliard . . . nor did I. What will she do? Take walks by that old river? That muddy old river.

Chase Jr. told Gavin . . . proudly . . . that after spring rains in the Virginia mountains, the Roanoke carries tons of Virginia topsoil through North Caro-

lina to the Albemarle Sound. Why does he think that is amusing? Now, here he is, a North Carolina small-town doctor carrying my angel daughter, the beautiful Saravette, off, in effect, down the same river to an edge-of-swamp town to live her life out as a country doctor's wife and helpmate, to bear and rear children by the same river, only muddier. He told Gavin, "In the spring, Mr. Whittington, because of your Virginia topsoil, our muddy old river turns the color of hoe-cake batter." Color of what? Ho what?

Chase certainly can be charming, sweet, respect-ful, down-to-earth, but he is from some other world, I do fear. Not Saravette's world . . . at all. Certainly, everyone who meets him likes him. Even loves him, young and old. And surely I shall also . . . if I can just forgive him for seducing . . . winning my little girl, my only child . . . who has been my life for twenty-two years. A quarter of a century, damn near!

My every thought and possibly more energy I've given to her than to . . . Gavin. Surely not. Well . . . have to think about that.

Mrs. Genevieve Whittington began weeping.

And the ceremony had not even started. Then came the handsome young groomsman, an attorney, Jeff Shannon from Williamston, to escort her.

The men and boys do look handsome in their gray morning suits. All at my insistence, of course. The high-noon wedding. Nothing more elegant when done right. Even those country boys look refined. Actually, young Mr. Shannon seems rather dashing, offering his arm to me, the bride's sniffling mother . . . well, I must stop. There's my music to proceed, "Sheep May Safely Graze." I cannot, must not, embarrass Gavin and Saravette by crying down the aisle. Dear God, help me!

Of all times! Dry me up. I must try to think of something dull, dreary. Maybe Father Simpson's sermons. Now, that would dry any eye! Any day except Sunday. Actually, Sunday, too. Some Episcopal priests, well many—her mind wandered, but she did stop crying—*are so darned afraid of offering any life, energy, enthusiasm, or God help us, emotion to their brief sermons; meant only to suggest, teach, to gently lecture, certainly not meant to excite, for which I am eternally grateful.*

Having stopped sniffling, she stood slowly, then gracefully accepted the arm of the nice young lawyer, Chase's friend.

He doesn't look country at all. He is perfectly at ease, confident, gently smiling, patting my hand just a bit. Why, he could have grown up here in Richmond!

Jeff escorted her to her pew, held her left hand until she was seated where Gavin would join her after he gave the bride away. After Father Simpson asked, "Who giveth this woman to this man?" Gavin would answer "I do" and join her.

Such a frightening thought, a father 'giving' his only daughter away.

She almost began to cry again. But, remembering Father Simpson's sermons and "Shalt nots," she dried right up.

Shalt not . . . shalt not . . . something or other.

She turned a bit to look at Chase's mother, Serena Haughton.

Quite attractive, Serena. We'll have them up here some weekend soon when something is happening at the club. My God, they're holding hands. Like kids.

Dr. and Mrs. Haughton. And smiling. Well, they have something to smile about. Chase making a catch like our girl. And here she comes. We shall all, the five hundred wedding guests, rise in respect for this bride who's headed for the swamps. My, she is beautiful. Her dad looks so proud . . . and humble, if that's possible.

Now what . . . what is she doing now? Looking into her bouquet, into one of the calla lilies . . . taking her arm away from her father and reaching into the lily and pulling something out. Smiling at her Daddy. Big smile. Now Chase and his father are walking out from the choir . . . room and she's smiling at him . . . big, and showing him something. This so is unlike Saravette to be carrying on silly during this serious moment. Has she lost her mind? Chase looks confused. Looking back and forth from the thing in her hand to her face.

And, my God, where are her shoes? What's wrong with her feet? What is she thinking? Is she thinking?

Genevieve turned around to see if other people noticed.

'Deed they did.

They were fascinated, stunned. All this activity

going on up at the altar. After some whispering among all concerned, Father Simpson, Estelle, Dr. Haughton, Chase, Saravette and Gavin . . . she put the item into her father's pocket, turned to the priest, and they all took a deep breath. And so, whatever it was . . . a mouse? . . . her wedding ring? No. That would be in Chase's pocket. A lucky penny she found? Well, Genevieve didn't feel like crying any more. She was mystified. Curious. Couldn't wait to get out of that church.

God, let this wedding end. Please.

Chapter Two

After the Honeymoon

St. Chanel.
Chanel No. 5.

Saravette reacted wistfully to the fragrance as it drifted up from her trousseau when she lifted the lid of her wedding-gift luggage. She was unpacking in Williamston, North Carolina, after a perfect honeymoon in New York City at the Waldorf. She and her new husband, Dr. Chase Haughton, Jr. had stepped down from the Atlantic Coast railroad car the night before at eleven o'clock at the old station into the arms of her new in-laws, Dr. Chase Haughton, Sr. and his wife, Serena.

Saravette and Chase spent their first night in Williamston in her new inlaws' guest room where,

apparently, they will have to remain until Chase finds them a house. He left her this morning, their first morning at home, at 7:30, rushing out of the house with his father for his first day at work as a doctor, the culmination of years of planning.

"I'll be home for lunch!" he called to her, walking backwards down the walk, stars in his eyes and his Daddy's old white medical jacket over his arm. He had not kissed her good-bye.

"No, they won't," said Serena, peering out the door with her arms crossed over her breasts. "They're like children at Christmas, finally working together after all these years. You've heard, of course, how Chase hovered about his Daddy's office every minute he wasn't on the football or baseball field or on the basketball court. He never had much time for girls, you know."

"Oh, now, that's not what I heard, Mrs. Haughton. They certainly were chasing him at Davidson, according to my cousin, Jack, who was his fraternity brother. And when I met him while he was at medical school in Richmond, I saw myself how girls were

chasing Chase. I'm surprised he ever noticed me."

Serena smiled at her new daughter-in-law, having liked her from the first day they met. "Oh, here now, girl. You don't have to be self-effacing to me. Everybody knows what a catch you are, young lady. Considering your reputation in Richmond, we were surprised you agreed to marry Chase and live in a small country town outside nowhere in particular, halfway between Raleigh and Nags Head and halfway between Norfolk and New Bern."

They strolled back down the hall to the kitchen where Serena made coffee. Saravette thought Serena was delightful, for a mother-in-law.

"Oh thank you, Miz' Serena," smiled Saravette, appreciating the humorous description. "I was wondering where in the world Williamston was!" She was truly wondering, however, what Mrs. Haughton meant by "your reputation." So she asked her.

"Oh, you know what I meant, honey. You were so popular and well-liked, talented, dated so many boys from the best families. Led the deb ball. They must all be wondering how you ended up halfway between . . ."

Saravette helped her finish, "Raleigh and Nags Head and halfway between Norfolk and New Bern. But Miz' Serena, that's not exactly the way it was. All that 'well-known, popular' business."

"Oh, really? Then how was it? What was it all about?" asked Serena.

When Saravette hesitated, "Well, it seemed to me to . . . ," Serena interrupted.

"Oh, that's all right, honey. I didn't mean to pry. You don't owe me an explanation. I was being rude. But you do please me when you don't call me 'Mrs. Haughton.' Just plain 'Serena' will do fine. I could relax better if you weren't so formal."

"I'll try, Mrs. Haughton. Uh, Serena." Both winced and smiled.

"Saravette, I do hope you're prepared for how different it will be here for you, for anybody who grew up in a city. Richmond we are not."

"Oh, yes. My mother said the same thing. She tried to prepare me. She grew up in a small town on the eastern shore of Virginia, so Richmond was a real chore for her at first, to learn their ways."

"Did your mother think you'd have a hard time adjusting to small-town people? "

"Oh, not to the people, Mrs. Haughton. However, she did say she wished I could live here a year before I decided to live here the rest of my life. Wasn't she silly? She must have known I'd live anywhere Chase wanted to go."

"Your mother is smarter than the average bear. To realize . . . "

"She's what?" asked Saravette.

"Oh, I don't mean your Mama is a bear, honey. That's just an old Martin County expression. Look here. You need to get unpacked. You go ahead and get started. There's an extra closet for you in the back hall. I'm running to town a minute. Just a block away, you know." Laughing again. "Got to find my keys. I'm always losing my car keys."

"Are you driving to town?"

"That's right. One block. Isn't that dumb? Nobody here walks anymore. Having a car at the door has ruined us all."

"Well, everybody drives in Richmond, too. Everywhere."

"Of course they do. In Richmond, it's a long way everywhere. Unlike here. And I always got lost in Richmond. Did I tell you my little sister finished at St. Catherine's? But here, do go on and unpack, now. I'm gone."

Left alone, Saravette went down the hall to the back bedroom, one of only three in the one-story "bungalow" house Doc had originally built right after World War I to house teachers. It was even called "The Teacherage." The Haughtons had reared Chase and his sister, Mary Cavette, in the largest mansion in town, "Monkey Top Two" on Main Street. Then when Mary Cavette's little boy, Danny, started school, Serena insisted her daughter move out of the old renovated tenant house that sat on Serena's family farm and come to town to live in the "Big House," so Danny could walk to the Church Street School.

She and Doc were ready to give up the big house and "trim down," she told everybody. She wanted a smaller house, all on one floor, "to make life simpler." But Serena had not slowed down one bit. She still

spent her summers at The Arlington Hotel at Nags Head, continued to go to New York on a train two or three times a year for shows and shopping with a group of women where they did not waste a minute. From all over Northeastern North Carolina, they came to ride the train to New York, playing bridge, comparing notes on clothes and recipes—a joke among them, as none were ever caught perspiring over a hot stove—and continuing the camaraderie of their summers at Nags Head.

Saravette never expected, however, to be living with Chase's parents. This was not how she had pictured anything. No sir, not at all. She had every reason to believe they would start off in their own house, no matter how small.

Gently from her trunk she lifted out silk blouses and hosiery, a church suit she had worn with a matching hat, gloves and shoes for her "going-away" outfit. She remembered a joke her mother had told everyone in Richmond and Charlottesville.

"How do you know you are at a Southern wedding? Easy. The bridesmaids' shoes are dyed to match the punch."

Especially amusing since that was just what happened at her wedding. Her mother and the wedding planner at Thalheimer's decided everything. She smiled and went along with it all. It made no difference to her as long as Chase showed up as the groom. This year, 1940, the most elegant color, in Richmond anyway, was pink. Pink this, pink that, pink flowers, dresses, punch, even lavalieres. So Mrs. Buckhauser, the wedding planner, whom Gavin called "Mrs. Buckspender," said, "We certainly don't want Saravette Whittington's wedding to be just like everyone else's. Absolutely not. We'll use a much more refined, elegant color, mauve. All mauve."

And mauve it was. Only my dress was not mauve, it was candlelight satin—more like "coffee-with-lots-of-cream," Mrs. Buckhauser said. Mauve flowers, mauve bridesmaids' gowns, mauve shoes, mauve-colored pearl ear drops I gave each girl as a gift, mauve champagne punch with mauve-colored frozen violets floating in the punch.

I didn't even like mauve. But what could I say? I saw my mother and Mrs. Buckhauser asking, "So.

What color would you like then, Saravette?" looking at me as blank-eyed as two parrots.

If I'd suggested, "Blue, maybe? Sky blue?" they likely would have said, "Blue! Nobody gets married in blue. It's a sad, tired color. Haven't you ever heard the expression, 'I feel so down and blue, I'm just singing the blues'?" And they would have laughed at me. I can hear it in my sleep.

And if I'd suggested green . . . They'd have come up with something like, "You mean olive green or slime green? Or the green color old cheese turns in the ice box or grass green or deep forest green or Christmas green?" and one would have said, "She got so sea-sick she turned green. Saravette, you mean that green? Darlin', you just stick to your piano, honey, and let us, your family, plan colors and everything for your wedding. You never even played with dolls when you were little. Always reading or playing the piano. How can you suddenly up and start doing things you've had no practice for? Really!"

She began to lift out petticoats, many in mauve, of course, and one of the fourteen nightgowns she

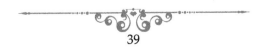

had received at her lingerie shower. *A different night-gown for every night of our first fortnight together. I wonder who in the world ever dreamed up that notion. Who could possibly use fourteen nightgowns? Seven for winter and seven for summer? Seems silly.*

As she glanced into the Chippendale mirror hanging above the walnut dresser, she jumped to see someone else staring back at her, too. She clutched a mauve petticoat to her chest and gasped.

The figure reflected in the mirror was a large black woman, arms crossed, unsmiling, since she saw very little to smile about, standing in the door-way and watching Saravette unpack. She had no idea how long the woman had been standing there, leaning on the door jamb, regarding her . . . .

And that was Saravette's first encounter with Beulah Bazemore, Miz' Boo, the long-time maid for the Haughton family.

As she watched silently, Boo was worrying to herself, *Lord God! This baby's gonna' surely need some watchin' over, from You . . . and from me.*

Chapter Three

Saravette's First Visitors

⎯◦ Betty Ann ◦⎯

*B*oo answered the door one morning and came back with a young woman. "Miz' Haughton, this is Betty Ann Shannon to see you. She's an old friend of the family."

Saravette was pleased to see a girl about her age and invited her to sit down. "Boo , would you please bring us some iced tea?"

Betty Ann sat down, saying, "You probably don't remember me from the party the Haughtons gave you before you were married and we barely shook hands

at your reception in Richmond, but I've been looking forward to welcoming you to Williamston. As Boo said, my family are old friends of the Haughtons."

"That's wonderful," said Saravette. "I'm so glad you came by. How long have you known Chase and his family?"

Betty Ann laughed. "Actually, ever since we were born. He and I were in kindergarten, primary and high school together. My father is the attorney for the Haughton family." And, she added, "Except they seldom need an attorney because they never get into trouble!

"You'll enjoy Williamston. We have a lot of clubs here and you might want to join some of them: the music, garden or book clubs? And will you be going to church with Chase at First Presbyterian?"

Saravette ventured, offhand, "I assume so, although I grew up in St. James Episcopal Church."

"I understand you enjoy tennis, but we don't have a club here in Williamston yet. I do have friends I can call in Little Washington, just twenty-four miles away."

Betty Ann's "bad angel" on her left shoulder

laughed, "That will get her out of town and away from Chase occasionally, and it may even annoy him." The "good angel" on her right shoulder reminded her to treat Saravette with the ladylike manners she was trained to use when she was a debutante. Truth to tell, the "bad angel" was talking a little bit louder . . . .

Saravette enjoyed Betty Ann's visit and invited her back.

⟿ Ham ⟾

"Just call me 'Ham,' honey. Everyone else does. Hammond is such a mouthful." The tall, handsome man marched through the Haughton's hall to the sitting room. "I'm the organist at the 'pistopal church. I hear you play piano and organ." Big smile.

"You mean to tell me you are the organist at the church and your name is actually 'Ham'? I can't believe you. Surely you lie. Did they name the Hammond organ for you?"

"Ain't it hell?" And he smiled, making her feel more at home than she had since arriving in Williamston.

Boo brought in some iced tea spiced with local apple cider and some of her hot-out-of-the-oven cheese straws and sat down to visit with Ham. He made her do it.

"Hey, Miss Beulah, our Miz' Boo. Sit down and tell us, this girl here and me, just exactly what is going on in Williamston. We needs to know."

"Oh do, Boo. I didn't know you were the town gossiper," laughed Saravette, getting excited at the prospect.

"I ain't no gossip, now, you hear?" smiled Bo.

Ham interrupted, "Oh no, she's no tell-all. She just knows all. But she keeps it to herself."

"Then why do you think she'll tell anything juicy to you and me?"

"Because Boo has a built-in lightning rod that warns her what can be repeated and what can't. What is harmless fun and what won't bear repeating. It's a gift. She was born with it. Like that other gift." Ham winked at Boo. "The reason all the young

women try to avoid her."

"Gracious, what could that be?" Saravette was wide-eyed now.

Ham and Boo regarded her. Ham changed the subject. "Darlin', where in hell did you get that name of yours, 'Saravette'? I've never heard it before in my whole life."

Boo went back to the kitchen.

"Surely you can guess, Ham. I'll give you one try. No more."

"All right. One guess. You are named for two grandmothers, one from each side."

"Now that wasn't so hard, was it?"

"Nope. One was obviously Sara."

"Correct. And the other?"

"Got me. Marriette? Georgette? I know, Babette! That has to be it. Babette! Like in the French novel. . . . or that famous prostitute in New Orleans. I can tell by your face. It's Babette!"

"You nut! No, no, no. It was my grandmother on my father's side, Juliette."

"Why, of course. Sara and Juliette came together

as Sara . . . okay. Now, girl, where did that 'V' come from? No 'V' in Sara nor Juliette. I'm not that dumb. I can see that 'Saraette wouldn't do. Saravette does read better, and even sounds better . . . but the V?"

"Ham, you are so silly for a grown person. Who cares where my name came from?"

"Well, obviously I do."

Beulah heard Saravette laugh out loud for the first time since she had been in this house. She took note and had to listen from the dining room door.

"Ham, it's so simple. In my family, at least. My father said, 'Keep it simple . . . just throw a V in the middle to pull it together. Take the V from our beautiful state of Virginia, named for the Virgin Queen of England by Sir Walter Raleigh.'

"Oh, but then my mother didn't care for it. Thought it was too cute and might cause a lot of questions, such as yours. She preferred old-family, safe names like Elizabeth, Katherine and Mary."

"So, she was just an ol' stick-in-the-mud. Didn't like anything different and unusual."

"Well, sort of. But she gave into him after he told

her about that Royster man in Raleigh who named all his children for original states of the union: Carolina, Georgia, Virginia, Vermont. In fact, Vermont Royster is writing for the *Raleigh News and Observer* as we speak, and some say he has a great future in journalism."

And so it went. Finally, before Ham left and she thanked him for the gardenias, he told her he had a matter he wanted to discuss with her. He did. Then he left.

Saravette gathered together the tea things, the left-over lemon slices and cheese straws, and carried them back to the kitchen, where she asked Beulah, "Boo, what is Ham's wife's name? I never heard him mention her."

Boo kept wiping the stove top. "Honey, Ham ain't got no wife. Never will have."

"Why not?"

"Well, he don't want one." She looked Saravette straight in the eyes, as if to say, "You understand?" Then she continued, "Okay, now tell Ol' Boo what it was he wanted to discuss so seriously with you that he lowered his voice."

"Oh, nothing serious. I don't know why he lowered his voice. Did he do that? *How did she hear that?* Anyway, a couple of things. He heard I played piano and a little organ and he asked me to fill in for him sometimes, like one Sunday every six weeks so he can have a weekend off to visit friends and relatives."

"Well, my," said Boo. "How about his Mama's florist business? He plays for weddings and funerals, but he makes his real living off doing church flowers on Sundays all over town and providing flowers for the weddings and funerals he accompanies on the organ. I guess he's got that trade all wrapped up."

Chapter Four

Adjusting to the In-laws' House

September 1, 1940

"Well, sugar, I gotta get back to the office. We have a full afternoon. I don't know how Daddy did it, I swear, all by himself. They're comin' out of the woodwork . . . and he's got to go out in the country this afternoon, so I'll be by myself. I'll be in the country a good part of tomorrow." Looking pointedly at her, "I know you're surprised by house calls. They certainly don't do too much of that in Richmond anymore . . . but folks have taxis and buses. These people, many of them, don't even have cars, or they're too sick to move."

"Isn't Williamston large enough to have a hospital?"

"Maybe, someday," he smiled, "but, so far, we are . . . it."

"You really like being needed, don't you, Chase?"

He thought a minute, shrugged his shoulders. "Maybe. I don't know. Look, honey, Miz' Messick will be wondering where I am."

"But, Chase," she reached for him. "When do you think? . . . my piano is stored out there in the damp barn . . . ." That stopped him.

"Oh . . . that's it. That's what you're really missing, isn't it?"

"Of course not, but our own place!" she said. "And," she whispered, ". . . and some privacy." He looked out the window and nodded slowly. "Well, that Jones baby ought to be . . . how old now? I'll see if I can get Daddy to speak to them about moving on out of Mama's tenant house . . . to somewhere—"

"Looks like I'm the only one interested in moving . . . you don't seem to care."

"No, baby, it's just . . . moving. I do hate to move. All that packing, rearranging, hauling, sorting, deciding . . . what to take. What not. Hire a truck. Hire

men. Who do we trust with the wedding gifts . . . not to break or steal them, like all that flat silver? I know you love that Old Maryland engraved design." He smiled. "Will the well water be clean enough for you out there? Will you miss being near people and living one block from downtown here?"

"Chase, stop it. The problem is—that right now, I do understand that you're concerned only with getting your work off to a good start with your daddy. I know that you have a calling and you're answering it." She paused. "I'm afraid you shouldn't have gotten married yet . . . better to have waited a while."

He looked rather helpless through all that . . . but also, he needed to leave, and she saw that.

"Before you get away, one more little thing . . . you're going to be a father."

Chase sucked in his breath. "We've only been married a few weeks!" he shouted.

That was the wrong thing to say.

"A few weeks! It's been three months! Since June first. Twelve weeks. Ninety days!"

"Oh, God. I didn't mean to sound that way . . .

I'm thrilled, darling, honest I am. We're just not . . . settled yet. I have to get used to the idea, I guess. I'd thought we might wait a bit. Certainly until we had a house."

"You-told-me-we-had-a-house. To move straight into. Right on the edge of town, a quaint old tenant house where Mary Cavette and Big Dan had lived until little Danny was born. Now they're living in your parents' big, ten-room house . . . and they have only one child. No more came along . . . but I don't want their big house, or anything huge like that . . . just our own place, for us and the baby. And now that I'm expecting, after what you said, maybe you and your Daddy won't want me to move, either . . . but darling, we must. You may have to take a week off . . . ."

"A week! Good Lord! I just started! And we took a week off for us to go to New York . . . on that honeymoon . . . ."

"Ooh, on 'that' honeymoon? Was it that bad? I thought you liked it. After all, your parents gave it to us . . . sent us . . . sent us up there on the train. Why

did I think it was so wonderful and you did not?"

He came to her. "Oh yes, honey. It was wonderful. Sweetest week I ever had. And your parents gave us a week at the Waldorf and the champagne. *And it's a wonder we didn't get a baby* that week! We are so spoiled." He smiled.

"And Doc and Serena gave us the tickets to two plays and the opera. How can you call it . . . 'that' honeymoon?"

"I swear, it was a slip. I just feel guilty after telling Daddy for so long . . . hold on . . . as soon as I get out . . . as soon as I pass exams, I'll be there. The week in New York with you was, so far, baby, the highlight of my life. You know it was. It's just to take another week off to move six blocks? But I know you need to have your own place. I have been . . . I'm sorry . . . thoughtless. I thought you and Mother were having such a good time together, got along so well . . . I just let it slide. I certainly have been remiss. We'll do something . . . tomorrow. No, I'll be in the country tomorrow. Surely the next day." He started to the door. Then turned.

"Have you been enjoying your tennis games over in Little Washington?"

"You have to go. And now, I guess I'll have to give them up."

"Oh, you can keep up a few more months. The newer way is for expectant mothers to stop just sitting down and 'resting' all the time, not good for all the muscles. They put on pounds. You need to walk, walk, walk and a few games of light tennis won't hurt you. That's old wives saying to 'take it easy' all the time. You're going to be the healthiest new mom in town . . . and he'll be the healthiest baby."

"He?"

"Another slip. We'll talk tonight. I'm off. Congratulations, sugar." He kissed her. And squeezed her. Looked at her and burst out laughing.

"Gee, what's so funny?"

"You are. We are. The whole damn thing. Takes a fella back . . . how fast things come along . . . after years . . . years of school, interning, exams . . . wedding, 'that' trip to New York, new job, new office, new nurse, new . . . real, live patients, new house,

live baby, . . . and a new wife. And what a wife!"

"You get tired just thinking about it, don't you?" Saravette said, smiling.

"Tired? . . . No, not tired. Excited, certainly. Feel like I'm in the middle of a whirlwind."

"Maybe a hurricane?"

"But how do you feel about it?"

"I don't even know. I've hardly met all the people in Williamston, yet. I don't know how to cook . . . 'boil water,' yet . . . I haven't even made a bed. Boo does it every day before I can get to it."

"Oh yes you have, my darlin'. You've made a bed. *Your* bed."

"And now I must lie in it."

"But you're going to do all right. To be all right. You'll be a wonderful mother."

". . . and wife?" She raised her eyebrows.

"And especially wife," he smiled broadly, rubbing her shoulders.

She turned her head and kissed his right hand, insisting, "Hurry now, Miz' Messick will be worried. She's too good a nurse to lose."

He hugged her good, and winked on the way out. "We'll move out there soon, I swear." And he was gone—again.

The telephone rang while Saravette was sorting boxes of wedding presents in preparation for the big move six blocks away. The little tenant house sat just outside the edge of town on the farm Serena Haughton had inherited, next to a cotton field where Williamston stopped. The house was located under four giant oak trees whose shade kept it cool in the summer. After the leaves dropped in the fall, the sun warmed the house in winter. Saravette raked leaves for the first time in her life and raked and raked. Chase put a stop to that, however.

"Wait a minute, baby. Walking, light tennis, with good tennis shoes, that's one thing. Raking, that's quite another. By the way, does anybody here in Williamston play tennis? Would any of them drive over to Washington with you?"

"Not that I know of. But I don't know many people. Betty Ann says she knows of no one, either."

"Do you see her often?"

"Not really. She works for her father, you know."

"Has she included you in anything? Or her mother? Or offered to have a party?"

"They haven't done that yet, but they've been very nice. Both asked me to play bridge with their clubs, but I don't play."

"Neither do I. Never had time. There's a men's poker club here, but I probably won't do that, either. Haven't played since undergrad."

Serena walked in on this. "Now, the Music Club, honey. That's what you ought to join. I'm not in it, but I'm not musical and I don't even sing in the choir, but I think I'll call Miz' Bradberry. She's president, or used to be."

"Oh, Miz' Serena. Don't bother with that. If they want me in, they'll call."

"Well, my darlin'! Not many of the members know you and none of them have heard you play. Of course, they have a membership limit so they can

stay small enough to meet in their homes . . . or some such reason. But they may not be full. Chase says you're looking forward to having your piano out of storage."

"Oh, I am. Dr. Lawton, my teacher at home, says I must stay in shape."

"What for?"

"Well, he said I'd probably be asked to do some concerts down here."

"In Williamston?" asked Serena. Except for the annual children's recitals . . .

"I think he mentioned possibly Raleigh, Wilmington, Norfolk, perhaps for the Music Department at East Carolina Teachers' College over in Greenville."

Serena and Chase looked at one another.

Chase asked, "Who is supposed to arrange these recitals?"

"I really hadn't thought of that. He must have assumed . . . that you would."

"Me? Us?" said Chase. "I didn't know anything about this. I've only heard you play twice . . . and Mother never has. Have you done these concerts

before, while you were at Juilliard?"

"Yes."

"Were you paid?"

"Yes."

"How much?"

"Not so very much, this early. Some were done for charities, for churches. I was just getting started."

"Honey, I'm sorry. I just didn't know you planned to do concerts down here."

"Had you thought about teaching?" asked Serena. "But of course Sally Manning and Mrs. Cone already have most of the students tied up, I'm afraid."

"Actually, I would be more interested in teaching over at the college, but expecting this baby . . . that may not be a good idea."

Serena nodded and left the room. "I'm going to call Miz' Bradberry right now, dear."

"Saravette, I wasn't aware you were still thinking of doing concerts. Maybe we should check out hiring a manager who could organize these things, the pay arrangements, all that." He looked worried. "I knew you were very good. I think I remember

hearing you were on the cover of a magazine one time as a child prodigy of the year."

"Yes, *Look* magazine."

"I bet you were pretty."

"Well, Mother liked it. And Daddy."

"When can I hear you play?"

"When we move in and get the piano tuned."

"Does a piano really have to be tuned every time it's moved?"

"Oh, yes. But the change of temperature and atmosphere is even worse . . . from damp to dry, hot to cold."

"My, they're temperamental."

"Oh, yes."

He couldn't resist. "Like some pianists I know?"

"How many do you know?"

"Sugar, the only one I want to know. The only one."

"You really don't know any other musicians?"

"Well, of course, our organist at First Presbyterian and Hammond Fletcher who plays over at the Episcopal Church and Elizabeth Fuller at the Baptist Church. She's very good, they tell me. Honey, all

church organs sound alike to me. Sorry."

Serena came back in with a worried look on her face.

"What's the news with the old Music Club, Mama?"

"Well, Mrs. Bradberry just said there had only been one opening and they filled that last week. Somebody's cousin moved to town."

"Is she musical?" asked Chase.

"It seems, not musical at all. Mrs. B. wasn't sure how she got in, or who put her up. I don't even know if Saravette's name was mentioned."

Boo came in from the dining room, polishing cloth in her left hand. "You know most everybody in that club, Miz' Serena. Somebody surely should put up this girl. She's the only real pianist in this town."

"Well, the truth is," Serena said thoughtfully, "I think most of the members are choir members. Very few, if any, are serious pianists. Ham can't be in it because he's a man and this group is part of the Woman's Club. Oh, maybe that's the problem here, Saravette. You're not a member of the Woman's Club yet."

"Do I have to join the Woman's Club? What is that? I mean, what do they do?"

"Well, I'm a member . . . a sometimes member. A supporter. Oh, they do different things. Something for everyone. Serve suppers. Have meetings."

"Well, with the baby on the way and our moving soon, maybe I won't join anything now."

Chase had left the room when his father called him to listen to the radio, Benny Goodman and his Orchestra playing "Tea for Two." Doc liked to tap dance to it.

"Are you a member of anything else?"

"I'm still a member of the Richmond Junior League."

"Oh, nice, honey. But can you work with that from here?"

"Oh, dear, I guess not. I'd better write them to take me off the list. Or give me a leave of absence . . . or something. And I'm a member of the National Music Teachers' Association. I qualified to teach while I was at Juilliard. But I believe you said there isn't a need for another teacher here. Now. Anyway, I'll be busy moving and getting organized."

Saravette left the room to continue packing more

wedding linens, to decide what to use and which to send back to her mother. And what about her silver? Flatware? Sterling tea service?

Serena went to the kitchen to ask Boo, "Is it just me or have only a few people called on Saravette, to visit her? I'm out and about so much, so I haven't noticed many."

"Some. Not many. Pretty much just Miz' Betty Ann Shannon, Jeff's sister, but she works at her daddy's office. When they do come, now that you mention it, they just drop in on Wednesday mornings, but that's when she's over in Washington, playing tennis. They say they're sorry they missed her, leave their card in the bowl over there . . . and go home." Boo smiled and said, "They feel they've paid their respects to the new bride."

"Why do they just come on Wednesday mornings?" Serena asked quizzically. Boo shrugged.

"But she has been asked to play bridge, right?"

"Yes'm. But she don't like to play. Or don't know how."

"Well, I'll have to teach her."

Boo didn't answer.

Serena looked to the ceiling and wondered aloud, "Maybe I abandoned her. Left her too soon, by going to the Arlington at Nags Head all summer."

"That's the hotel where my brother, Ben-Olive, cooks, isn't it?"

Serena nodded.

"She didn't want to go down with me and leave Chase. But she could've learned bridge down there."

"If she **wanted** to," offered Boo.

"But she really preferred to stay here with Chase and Doc, didn't she?" Serena added.

"Do you blame her, Miz' Serena? She just got married."

"She could've met a lot of people down there at the Arlington."

"I'll bet that's not what she got married to do."

Serena looked at Boo inquiringly. Boo quickly added, "You and Doc have been married a lot longer. A lot longer . . . but I do kinda' wonder how those people happen to drop in to see her most always on Wednesday mornings, when she was playing tennis over in Little Washington."

"Has she made friends over there?"

"I don't know. None to bring home. She said their team is going to play in a tournament one Sunday soon over in Greenville and others in Wilson and Rocky Mount. I kinda' get the idea the Washington crowd is tickled to have her, as she can help them win those matches all around."

"But she'll have to give it up soon."

"Miz' Haughton, some farm women keeps on working right on up 'til the baby drops out, which sometimes happens right out in the field where they're hoeing weeds or picking cotton." Boo kept drying dishes, putting them away.

"Well." No answer to that from Serena.

"And they're healthier for it and get well quicker after the baby comes, 'cause they didn't get so weak and flabby settin' around all dose months *before* the baby, doin' nothing, just getting' fat and tired. No wonder you white folks keep mamas in bed two whole weeks after the birth. They's so tired and weak—but it makes money for us nurses, like my cousin, Easter."

"Oh yes, I loved Easter. She was with me both times, for a month each, with Mary Cavette and Chase. Is she still nursing new mothers?"

"That she is. And will 'til she drops. She never sets down on a job."

"Well, I hope she'll be with Saravette. I better phone her about it."

"No problem, Miz' Serena. I arready done it."

"You have? When?"

"Five weeks ago."

"Before we knew?"

"That's right. I always know before you know. With both Mary Cavette and Chase, Jr., too."

"How can you tell?"

"By the mama's eyes."

Chapter Five

Saravette's "Best Friend"

The Phone Call

$\mathcal{B}$etty Ann Shannon phoned from Shannon and Clark law office. "Hey, sugar, how you feelin' after your move to that old tenant house?"

"Betty Ann, if anyone had told me how miserable this can be, I'd have paid someone else to do it."

"Do what, honey?"

"Carry this baby for me. I believe he's a football player, certainly a place kicker."

"Gosh, I didn't know it was that bad. What can I do for you?"

"Not a thing, I guess. Just listen to my complaining,

so I won't dump it on Chase. 'Course he's never here to hear it much, anyway."

"Oh, where is he?"

"You know, besides his office hours, he's trying to take some of the house calls off his daddy. He says Doc has been doing it all these years alone and he'd promised to relieve him and he's bound to it, which is good of him, I think. So like him."

"Well, isn't he ever at home, for meals, listen to the radio with you? Are you out there alone all the time?"

"Well, rather much, I suppose. Serena drops by and Mary Cavette. They send Boo out to help sometimes. 'Fraid I'll over-do it."

"Don't you have any real help at all?"

"Betty Ann, you know I don't need anybody. It's just the two of us. I'm trying to learn to cook and every cook I've been around never would let me in the kitchen."

"And you're not playing tennis with the group over in Washington or playing the organ at church anymore?"

"No and no. The tennis, obviously not . . . and

I just don't feel well enough to go to rehearsals Wednesday nights and play again on Sunday. Chase said something about low blood pressure, or high, I forget which, but it saps my strength. I hate it! I've never been sick before in my life! And, by the way, you're such a good listener. Sorry I poured all this on you, Betty Ann."

"Well, honey, it's the least I can do, listen, since there's nothing else you'll let me do for you. Can I bake you a pie?"

"Mercy, no! Everything makes me put on weight and takes my breath away. Thank you for the thought, tho'."

"Well, Chase could eat it, maybe."

"Oh, he doesn't eat sweets. Well. Rarely. If it was in the house, 'you-know-who' would eat it. It would sit in the icebox calling to me in the night 'til in a dream I'd float in there, in the dark, in my sleep, and eat it all up. I crave sweets! Why couldn't I crave celery, cucumbers, radishes?"

"I never heard of a pregnant woman who craved those things, sugar. But look, I'm going to book club

tonight. If we have an opening, do you think you'd like to be a member?"

"Oh, I'd love it! I love to read. Anything . . . and adore critiquing books. I read not only the backs of cereal boxes, but also the sides, bottoms, tops. Do get me in, would you? And I might meet a few more girls."

"That's what I was thinking. I'm sorry I haven't been able to do more for you like that. 'Course, there aren't too many girls here our age. The few that were, went off to work or school or marry and never came back, except for family reunions."

Saravette, changing the subject, asked, "So your father is the only lawyer in town?"

"Well, one of two. Just like Chase's daddy was one of only two doctors in town. But not anymore. We're all thrilled, tickled to death that Chase wanted to come home and practice with his daddy. Everybody loves Chase since he was a little boy. He is so much like Doc. Did you want him to stay in Virginia? In Richmond?"

"Oh, no. I wanted him to go wherever he chose. I can't really picture him liking a big-city practice in

Richmond. He prefers small-town life in every way."

"And how about you? Did you want to live in a town this small?" Betty Ann listened to Saravette very carefully.

"Oh, I'm sure I'll like it. I've barely unpacked my bags yet. I look forward to learning the town. Have you lived here all your life?"

"Every day of it. Just like Chase. We were always in school together, from kindergarten up. He was smart in school, as you would know, even though he played all . . . four . . . sports."

"I didn't know he played all four sports. What was there, besides football and basketball?" asked Saravette, wondering why he had never mentioned this to her.

"Well, my goodness! Baseball and track. The football coach required all his boys to go out for track in the spring, after basketball, to keep them limbered up for football season . . . or so he said. Ol' Coach Pat Thompson, my good friend. Thompson was the athletic director for the junior high and high school, and I volunteered in his office during

study hall my junior and senior years as his, sort of, secretary. Mama said I did it so I'd know everything going on and who made which teams, even before the boys knew!"

Saravette had never heard such talk as this girl gave. A whole different world: high-school sports. All she'd ever known was an all-girl prep school, St. Catherine's, and college at Juilliard. Also, studying for straight A's, piano and tennis practice, summers with family at Virginia Beach, and deb parties. Whenever she was required to take a phys ed course, she slopped through it good-naturedly, but when she had a choice, she always chose ballet because she liked the classical music she danced to . . . felt at home with it. Sometimes, she even accompanied the ballet classes on piano . . . fairly often, actually, now that she thought of it. When a large, hard ball of any kind was thrown at her . . . soccer, basketball . . . her instinct was to duck. Not tennis balls, of course.

"Betty Ann, I'm sure you played sports, too, didn't you? You look athletic."

Betty Ann laughed. "Oh, I don't know if I look it,

but I sure did love it, sports . . . every one they'd let me play. Basketball, softball, and track. Daddy said I had to have something for every season, to keep me out of the house . . . and Mama would add, 'You mean away from the stove, the dishes, and cleaning her room?' And then we'd all laugh, "HA-HA-HA."

"Sounds like your family had a good time."

"Lord, we did and do. I still live with them."

Saravette had wondered if Betty Ann was married, but hesitated to ask.

"And we all loved Chase and his family. We'd go down to Nags Head and our families would rent a house together for a week when we were children, climb the sand dunes, go fishing, crabbing. Doc Haughton and my daddy would cook up a big crab stew for about twenty people, if you count the children. Or we'd all stay at the old Arlington Hotel where Ben-Olive Bazemore cooks every summer. You know, Boo's brother. Oh, golly, I've had you on the phone too long. Bye now, see you soon."

Betty Ann went home from her father's office early, baked Saravette and Chase a chocolate pecan

pie with whipped cream topping and carried it to Saravette on her way to book club that night.

"Betty Ann, why did you do this? I thought you were my friend."

"Oh, honey, I knew you were joking . . . like you always do. And I remember it was Chase's favorite pie when he was a little boy and went to Nags Head with us. I could tell you needed cheering up. So let me run, hear?"

Saravette stood holding the pie and watched Betty Ann bounce gaily out to her Chevrolet sedan parked under the largest oak tree. Her heart sank. Chase was with his father having supper and dessert, if he wanted it, at Kiwanis Club, which met at the Boy Scout hut.

The Olde Roanoke Book Club

Mrs. Sadie Jones spoke slightly louder, just over the multiple conversations of a roomful of women, "Ladies, I know you're havin' fun chatting, but how

'bout we come to order and get started? This is our sixth meeting of 1940. Now, how many of you have read the chosen novel, *Gone with the Wind?*"

Five hands went up. Several said, "I've started it."

"All right, all right. We should be able to discuss it a bit. But first, Mrs. Sarah Harrison wrote this nice letter of regret saying tho' she has been a member for forty-nine years—imagine. Almost half a century . . . gracious! She doesn't get out at night anymore."

Somebody said, "We can give her a ride—take turns."

"Her evenings are set now to fit her pill schedule for her arthritis," explained Sadie. "She has supper at 6:00, puts the cat out, puts her gown on at 7:00, listens to the radio until 7:45, calls the cat in, goes to bed at 8:00. So, there you have it."

Silence filled the room.

"Lord, we have a lot to look forward to, don't we?" said Kitty Beale.

Again, silence echoed all around the room.

"And she didn't mention reading any books," someone offered.

"Her eyes won't let her anymore," Sadie responded.

Alice Mann insisted, "Hey, y'all, we really can take turns picking her up. She doesn't have to drive. My goodness, that's the least we can do for one of our first members . . . or new members, for that matter. Has anyone been in here longer than Miz' Harrison?" No one had. "Well, let's . . ."

"I already suggested that, Alice. I called her the minute I got her note. She said, 'No, no,' when I asked her."

"Well, all right then, who shall we get for the new twelfth member?"

"We asked Preacher Lindsley's wife once before, but she turned us down."

"She was expecting her second baby then."

"Maybe she's ready now."

"She's a good one, but how about that Perry girl over in Windsor?" offered Sally Jones.

"And maybe Doc Haughton's new daughter-in-law. Wouldn't she like to read?" asked Miz' Alice. Had anybody met her?

A few "yesses." One, "only at church."

"She turned down two bridge clubs. Doesn't like it," said Mary Ruth Bailey.

"And when Serena suggested she join the Woman's Club, she said, 'Do I have to join the Woman's Club?'"

"How do you know she said that?" asked Elsie Jones.

"I don't know," said Elsie, "I don't know where I heard that. But I didn't make it up and Serena didn't tell me."

"You know, somebody said that girl even named her piano! Elliot, Mr. Elliot." Everyone laughed. Almost everyone.

"Hey, Betty Ann? You know that Haughton girl right well, don't you?"

"Pretty well. Yes," murmured Betty Ann. "She's nice, I think. A great girl . . . ."

"Oh, that's what you always say. There's no point in asking you," Mary Smith laughed.

"Well, gee, I don't know about that, now," Betty Ann said.

"Well, we do. You never say anything bad about anybody. You're just no help at all."

Mary Ruth added, "Not to say anything bad about poor Chase's new wife, but I hear she's out there complaining all the time like gangbusters. Ain't nothing right. Gets on Chase for not being home more . . ."

"Well, he can't," offered Miz' Harrison. "Their patients have doubled since Chase, Jr. came home."

"Doubled? How come?"

"Don't you see? Serena told me, or Mary Cavette, or somebody. All the people out on the edge of the county who used to go to Washington, Plymouth or Greenville, even Scotland Neck and Windsor, are coming here to the Haughtons' now."

"How about that?"

"My stars!"

"Interesting."

"Good for them!"

"Well, y'all, if we're going to have time for dessert and coffee, we'd best tend to this voting business right away. How about Mrs. Lindsley, the Presbyterian minister's wife? Nobody'd object to her, would they? No objections?" asked Mrs. Alice Mann, gazing about the room, her eyebrows lifted.

"Alice, honey, you aren't even the president now, are you? Why don't we let our president do that, hear?"

"OK by me. She wasn't getting it done and I was about ready for Lily's 'Mile High' lemon meringue pie."

"Thank you, Alice," said Sadie. "I don't care who does this. I'm only president because you all insisted it was my turn. But if there are no objections, I'll call Lydia Lindsley tomorrow and ask her to join us as our newest member and to come to our next meeting."

"Fine, fine," they chorused. "And how about we enjoy our pie while we discuss this book, okay?" suggested Lucy Barnhill. There were no objections.

At first. But . . .

"Oh, now listen, y'all. Let's think about this a second." It was Alice Mann again. "Just thought of something. If Lydia has turned us down once, maybe we shouldn't go running back to her again . . . so soon. She was at Peace College with my sister, who says she's a great girl, but not inclined to read a whole lot."

Someone laughed. "And we are?"

But Alice went on, "Why don't we seriously consider that cute Perry girl from Windsor? She is just so much fun. She won't mind riding over here, just

nine miles, and we don't mind going to her house occasionally. Besides, her house is so unusual . . . full of off-beat antiques."

President Sadie said, "Sure thing. It's all right with me. I knew her at St. Mary's and everybody liked her," looking about.

They all quickly agreed, all talking at once.

"Oh, sure."

"Of course."

"OK by me."

"Why not? My husband hunts with hers."

"She's cute."

"Mary Lou takes piano lessons from her cousin."

"Why doesn't she take lessons here in Williamston? From Miz' Sally and . . . You drive all the way to Windsor?"

"You know," said another girl, "Windsor has always had more 'class' than Williamston."

"Well, by golly, I don't think so." Dropped jaws.

"Hey, here comes the pie."

One member merely watched, listened and smiled. Wanting to pat herself on the back, she ate only one bite of the 'Mile High' lemon meringue pie.

Chapter Six

Christmas

1940

*P*oor Saravette. Nauseated for three months. Still unsettled in the small former tenant house in the country, just outside of town, the house with no name, unlike old houses in Richmond. Her home in Richmond was "Piper's Hill" and Chase, too, grew up in a house with a name, "Monkey Top Two," in Williamston. But no name for this house . . . except, maybe, "Dinky." But she actually found it a perfect, neat, four-room house for a couple beginning their married life. Some couples had less space: two-room apartments, even one-room "studio" apartments, a nice name for a single room in New York.

Her savior, her piano "Elliot" or "Mr. Elliot," named when she was a young prodigy, was in his place in the living room—no one knew where the name came from, though one cousin in Richmond suggested that Saravette's mother had named it "Elliot" after a previous suitor of hers named Elliot Carstarphen, a musician, a pianist.

After ascertaining that he could not possibly support the former Genevieve Ashley in "the style to which she was accustomed," her family threw as much cold water as possible on that warm, budding friendship, without it seeming obvious, of course. Their efforts succeeded and the flame flickered out. Mr. Elliot left town for New York and his modest success there, considering he had no prominent family and few, if any, financial sponsors. He played Carnegie Hall once, accepted concert tours for some years, then ended up composing and teaching, married to another musician, a flutist.

Saravette's sterling tea service, inherited from her grandmother, was not unpacked. Nor was her silver dining candelabra. They had no dining room.

They ate in the kitchen. However, she insisted on using her sterling flatware every day, in every way. Anything was all right with Chase, Jr. He didn't care if he ate with his hands, because he was worried about that Griffin child's peculiar symptoms. He had gone through every medical book he and Doc could find to recognize the unusual combination of rash on the chest and midriff area, sore muscles, low-grade fever, red throat, no appetite, bouts of diarrhea, lethargy. No luck.

"I'm sorry, Saravette. I do recognize your symptoms. And there's not one sweet thing I can do about it except hold your hand when you lose your breakfast. I'm sorry you feel so sorry." She smiled. He smiled. "I wish I could take it over from you and be sick for you myself in your place. I've no idea why the Lord gave man only the pleasure and women the morning sickness. Soon she must birth the baby with great pain, feed it herself and often rear it alone while the male wanders off back into the jungle with the other cats, prowling about. Female tigers will bring the male tiger special food

surprises during their honeymoon, but after the kittens come, he's nowhere to be found. She has to do all that, too. Ain't fair, is it?"

"Gracious, Chase! I didn't ask for a zoology lecture. All I wanted was a little sympathy. I've never been sick in my life before. I don't know how to act. And you're never here to hold my hand, anyway. I'm too miserable to dress and go to any Christmas parties, especially alone. You're never available. I don't know the people, anyway."

And, she wailed, "I look so horrible. Bloated, face, hair impossible, eyebrows used to be . . . distinctive."

Chase threw in, "Magnificent, beautiful, and beguiling!"

"But, to me, today," she said, "they look . . . bushy, like they don't belong to me at all." She threw herself on the bed . . . sideways.

"Honey, just a few more weeks and it'll be all over. And what a prize we'll have!"

"A few weeks! Have you misplaced your mind? It's three more months! Twelve weeks 'til March.

You call that, 'just a few weeks'? Men kill me. If you were carrying it, throwing up, ankles swelling . . ."

"That's because you're not walking enough, sugar. How 'bout try walking three times a day . . . not too far, just enough to keep the circulation going. To keep your fluids from settling in your ankles and feet. I know you're tired of wearing those old slides around."

"Haven't been to church in weeks, no shoes to wear. I only played the organ three times for Ham . . . and had to stop."

"You miss your music, don't you?"

He thought she was going to cry, but she didn't, she never cried.

"You never cry, do you, baby? You are so strong. I am very proud of you, Saravette. You're like a pioneer woman, living out here in the sticks with none of the luxuries you're accustomed to. No servants. No lunches out. No tennis. No old friends. No music critics or teachers. No pleased fans after concerts . . . I did a bad thing, didn't I?"

She sat down . . . slowly, heavily, and looked up suspiciously at him.

"Bad? Like what?"

"Like asking you to marry me and move off down here away from your full life in Richmond." He leaned back on the mantle, his arms folded and his head slightly tilted to one side.

She folded her hands primly over her hard, swelled stomach, stared at the fireplace and thought a bit. "I didn't have to accept. I didn't have to come."

"Then why did you?"

"You know perfectly well why."

"Tell me."

"Because I loved you. Still do. You're the finest boy . . . man I've ever known, except for my father. I knew I'd go anywhere you wanted . . . needed to go. And I apologize for complaining. I really do. You do not deserve a complaining wife. You're a perfect man, a perfect gentleman. And there was no one like you in Richmond."

Chase was silent, obviously touched, deeply moved by her simple statement. Chase knew she believed it, meant it, but what he said, wagging his finger and smiling, was, "And don't you forget it!"

Then they hugged and laughed.

She grabbed her middle. She had felt an early, very early kicking movement. "Feel here, Chase." He did, and smiled. Saravette grimaced. "Wow . . . he . . . she . . . it . . . the baby heard what you said, too. And he's agreeing with his old dad, 'Mama, don't you forget it!'"

Another hug.

Then Chase rushed back to the office to see the Griffin boy and tell his father that he had not discovered anything new. They might need to carry him to Greenville, he told the father.

But the family had no car.

Chase decided to ask his mother, Serena, if she could spare her car and ask Ben-Olive Bazemore to drive the Griffin family to the Greenville Hospital Emergency Room, over in Pitt County.

Two-and-a-half months later in mid-March, Doc, Serena, Saravette and Chase also roared over to Greenville, twenty-five miles away, in Doc Haughton's Chevrolet for Doctor Pace to deliver Dr. Chase Haughton, Jr.'s new baby girl, Genevieve Whittington Haughton.

Chapter Seven

First Trip Back to Richmond

*T*hree months later, in mid-June, Saravette stared unblinking through the train's dusty window passing tobacco fields, green and hopeful, the main crop of ninety percent of these farmers. North Carolina was the leading tobacco state in the country and, one might say, a large producer of tobacco for the world.

She and Baby Ginny had been settled on the train at 8:00 that Tuesday morning by Serena, Chase, Doc, Boo and Ben-Olive, all looking strangely mystified about why she was taking their angel, their three-month-old darling, smiling already, away from

them to see her other grandmother in that stuffy old house in Richmond.

"How long will you be gone?" she was asked at least two dozen times at the station in Williamston by the Roanoke River in eastern North Carolina. "Why can't your mother come down here?" was asked only once as the answer invariably was, "She has a bad hip and can't travel."

"Can't we send some help there with you?" Boo was dying to go.

"No, mother has plenty of help. Thank you, tho,'" Saravette replied.

"Let me hold her one last time." From everybody, one last time, little Genevieve Whittington Haughton was snuggled, kissed, tickled, bounced. Saravette was afraid the baby would throw up from it or catch somebody's eastern Carolina sinus infection. *Do babies have sinuses?* she wondered.

"Here, take this bottle. You surely can't nurse her on that train."

"Oh, yes, I can. I'll just slip off to the ladies' room. Nobody'll see us in there."

"It's so small! You'll have to sit on the john!"

"Don't worry your head. Ginny and I'll do just fine."

Several others came to see them off, too. Hammond, the organist/florist; Chase and Doc's two nurses; Chase's older sister, Mary Cavette; her husband, Big Dan Hardison; and their son, Little Danny, on his way to Church Street School. Even Betty Ann Shannon, Saravette's "best friend." Betty Ann had brought her "something easy to carry," another hand-crocheted pink baby cap and a small book of eastern Carolina poetry for Saravette's mother, Miz' Genevieve, by a poet from Tarboro.

The porter was so solicitous, falling all over himself, trying to help with bags, the baby basket, offering to bring her something, anything, to make them more comfortable. The only thing she required was—could she please change to face front, and not ride to Richmond backwards?

"Oh yes, Miz' Haughton, absolutely!" Arrangements and changes were swiftly accomplished and she settled in, facing forward, adjusting the baby

first in her arms where she could smell the top of her head, kiss her tiny pink hands. And when Ginny fell asleep, place her gently in the basket beside her, cover her with the pink blanket Serena had knitted, the only item in God's world she had ever knitted. But she had been determined. "God, please help me finish it," she had prayed to her Lord.

Saravette turned to the window and the pine trees, pine trees and more pine trees rolling endlessly by, except for the ubiquitous tobacco fields interspersed with corn, cotton, old houses, mule sheds, pig sties, muddy roads and ditches.

Let's see now. What am I doing? Running away? Truth was, my mother had wanted to come to Williamston. Had a driver all lined up to bring her. . . . Planned to stay at the Tar Heel Hotel out of everybody's way for at least two weeks. After all, this was her first grandchild. She was happy to go around the world to see her, to hold her . . . certainly to Williamston, hip or no hip. She could carry the pain medicine with her, have Doc Haughton replace it, if necessary.

But I was adamant. I must, must go home. Discover why I want to cry all the time . . . but could not,

must not, let Chase see me cry. I never have. It is a point of pride with me. I am supposed to be strong, as he says. I never cry.

Of course, she did not plan to cry at her mother's house, either.

Ginny was nothing if not healthy, weighing nine pounds! Long, painful delivery. Miz' Easter, the old nurse, was with her for a month! Doc Haughton insisted. She usually stayed with mothers only two weeks.

Chase was thrilled. If he had ever preferred a boy, he never let it show. "Saravette, I love girls! What do you mean? Sure, I can play ball with her. Softball, and I'll take up tennis again. Remember, I played at Davidson? Maybe we can build our own family tennis court and all of us can play." His eyes lit up. They stayed lit up all the time. He talked of the future. "Should she go to St. Catherine's where you went, or to Mama's St. Mary's and maybe later, Sweetbriar or Agnes Scott . . . ?"

"Hey. Slow down, Chase. Let me enjoy her first before you send her off somewhere. Williamston

High School is fine! What would Miz' Ruth say if we sent her away?"

He couldn't hold her enough; burp her; change her didies; kiss her little fingers; gaze into her calm, wise blue eyes; sniff the top of her head; kiss her dimples.

"Saravette, did you have dimples when you were little?"

"Chase, you know very well I'm not the 'dimples' type. You have all the dimples in this family. Even that one on your chin."

My, he is handsome. I'm always amazed at how beautiful my husband is, yet he apparently doesn't even know it!

"You just snapped back like a rubber band," chirped Serena about Saravette's figure, almost back to normal.

"Nursing Ginny probably helps me lose weight, even tho' I'm drinking tons of milk."

"Oh, honey, you don't have to drink excessive milk to make milk," Serena said. "Remember, cows don't drink any milk a' tall and they make gallons of milk . . . from grass, weeds, corn, stuff . . . no milk."

Saravette's eyes opened wide. "Serena . . . you . . . are . . . right! I never even thought of that."

"God's just smarter than we are, darlin'. And your weight vanished because you were carrying a great deal of fluid. Did you use much salt? Doc says Chinese women inherently know that when they are carrying a child they should automatically swear off salt. But you do need some milk to get extra calcium for you both. Colonial women used to lose one tooth for every baby . . . well, I guess the poorer ones did . . . but lots of people back then lost teeth."

Serena rattled on. "That's one reason women used fans so much. So they could smile from behind their fans and hide the gaps in their gums. When out from behind the fans, it was customary for women to go about with their lips closed, and if they smiled at all, it was a tight-lipped smile as you often see in colonial portraits. Have you noticed?"

Saravette laughed. "Now that you mention it, most . . . in fact, all the women in the portraits in our house have tight-lipped expressions. I assumed all these women were just proud, serious, over-burdened,

patient matriarchs who had lost five of their ten babies, either in childbirth or later on from smallpox."

Both had agreed they were glad they lived now, not then. Serena was such good company, but she did go to Nags Head . . . all summer long. Why?

Even Saravette's famous, heavy, enchanting eyebrows, so like her mother's, began to look right again as her extra pounds fell away.

So why don't I look right? Feel right? I'm so tired! Tennis? I cannot lift a racquet. Maybe never again, feeling like this. Music? What's that? Play Grieg's Piano Concerto in A flat minor? I would fall off a bench instead of finishing his falling-down-the-mountain passage, and I could never complete those back-up-the-mountain runs. If I could play anything, it might be a bit of Beethoven's Moonlight Sonata or, especially, his Pathétique Sonata. I've tried to play Clementi's little Sonatina in C Major to cheer myself up. Even that didn't work, nor Chopin. I had thought about specializing in Chopin, as I'm never tired of him. Now, . . specialize in . . . what?

Even when I look at my precious girl, I feel, God,

I'm going to . . . cry! Because the baby is so innocent? Helpless? Or because I, her mother, feel so helpless? After all, this creature is not a tennis ball . . . nor a piano. Why in the world do I feel . . . all thumbs, except when I'm nursing her? Now, that is dreamy. I can close my eyes and drink in the love from my baby, just as she is taking nourishment from me. I can feel the love passing through my milk. I feel needed, needed and appreciated.

I cannot imagine the old-time mothers turning their babies over to a wet-nurse. How horrible. Those moms missed all the fun. Unless, of course, they had no milk. But sometimes, I've heard, they only wanted to avoid the whole business . . . get back into their party dresses . . . to the social whirl . . . and not worry about milk leaking through at feeding time, or having to run home from a party.

If I ever smiled these last three months, it was when I think of my baby, merely think of her and, suddenly, my arms would ache to hold her, my breasts tighten up, my milk comes in or comes down, as the old folks say, and I have to run, snatch up Ginny and

fall into position in my favorite rocking chair, given to us by Serena. The joy of it! The mystery of it. So. Why does that not extend to the rest of my life?

Ginny was waking up and fidgeting in the basket beside her and, as she lifted her out, the porter approached. "Miz' Haughton, when lunch is served, would you prefer to go to the dining car during the first seating at twelve o'clock, or the second one at one o'clock?"

"Oh dear, thank you. Either time, but I prefer the one that is less crowded."

"Fine, fine. I'll come and tell you when it's best," the porter said.

She nodded toward the baby and said, "I might be in the ladies'."

"Oh, yes. Very good, Miz' Haughton." And he vanished.

How did he know my name?

Mother had suggested she get a private compartment. "Mother, I didn't even think about it and it's too late now."

"I don't know why you insist on traveling second

class, third class."

"I'm not insisting, mother. I just don't care. Please worry about something else."

"Such as what?"

Saravette had no answer.

Nor did she today, either, looking out the window at unending pine trees.

Does Chase need me at all? He might have married anybody in the world because what he really cares about are his precious patients. They may need him, but not much more than he needs them. He wants and has a need to save them all.

My Lord, have I married a missionary? My psych teacher had said, "Watch out for a man with a mission. He won't be hanging around the house." That surely describes Chase.

She almost broke out in a sweat.

Did he feel he had to come home as the great healer? To do even more wonderful healing than his father had? What does he expect of me? A perfectly manicured house? No. He never notices. Delicious cuisine? Chase says, "How about some good ol'

Campbell's tomato soup and a grilled cheese sandwich, honey—maybe in the frying pan with a brick on it to help the cheese melt better?" That makes him happy as any fancy meal. He loves a big bowl of apples handy so he can grab one leaving the house. He truly is a love, so easy to please. He seems to enjoy my cooking efforts, like my chicken, soups, and cookies.

And in bed. In our special times, when he didn't fall asleep from exhaustion, he was a genius . . . gentle, patient, sensitive, a true gentleman lover, if there is such a thing. If he had been anything else, rough or crude, I would have quickly failed as a wife. Little Ginny was, indeed, a 'love child' . . . in the truest sense of the word.

Several people in the car seemed to want to make eye contact, as if hoping to chat, "ooh" and "aah" over the baby, or sit across from her and Ginny. She remembered what her mother had said, "Never make eye contact with strangers in public places." She did not explain why. Anyway, Saravette wanted no company. Not today.

At the station in Richmond, Mother Genevieve had arranged for a driver to pick them up, using a hand-made sign that read "Mrs. Haughton." This worked well and, after a short drive up Marshall Street, the man was helping her and the baby go up her mother's walk as servants were coming out to help, all aglow. Before she handed Baby Ginny to her delighted grandmother Genevieve, Saravette felt she was imploding . . . suddenly, tears, sobs, she couldn't control. She could hardly breathe.

"Darling! Saravette! What's the matter? Come into the sitting room right now." She put the baby back in the basket and the maid whisked her down the hall. She put an arm around her daughter's shoulders and led her straight to the sofa. "Here's a handkerchief. I've never seen you like this. Is there something you need to tell me?"

Saravette collapsed into herself. She could not speak for sobbing. She fell over sideways on the couch and gave in to her attack of tears in total abandon. They came from deep, deep, deep, from so long in the making, she could not possibly hold

them in. Besides, they . . . felt . . . so . . . good.

Dr. Trodden had already been called and was on his way, as was her father from the bank. Gavin rushed into the room and fell to his knees by her side. "Baby, what is it? Aren't they treating you right down there?"

She slowed her hysteria at the sight of her father. "Daddy, don't you want to see the baby?" she sobbed. "She's grown since you saw her." He and Genevieve had come to Williamston for a weekend right after Ginny was born and planned to come back for her baptism, later in the summer.

"Oh, I'll see the baby, darlin', but what is this with you? What can we do?"

"Nothing . . . nothing!" she wailed, starting in again, she threw her arms around her Daddy. "I'm so embarrassed to frighten you. I don't know what is wrong with me!" and she fell back down on the sofa in another spasm of sobs.

Genevieve and Gavin stood looking at her help-lessly, Genevieve wringing her hands, he with his arms hanging useless by his sides.

"When is that damn doctor getting here? They're never around, by damn, when you need 'em." He seldom cursed in front of his daughter, but . . . . He started over to pour a drink at, not a bar, but a bottle and glasses hidden down in the bookcase. Genevieve would never allow a wide-open "bar" in her house. A story went around that he kept a bottle in the back of the commode, just off their bedroom. Not that he was a lush . . . but occasionally a fella' might need a toot, even in this well-ordered house.

However, Piper's Hill was not well-ordered at this moment. The baby, Genevieve Whittington Haughton, was squalling at the top of her lungs, red in the face, barely able to catch her breath. The maids stared on helplessly and looked about for a bottle or a can of milk . . . or what?

Out in the hall, the cook Violet Mae said, "Miz' Saravette don't want no bottle to touch her lips. She's breast-feedin' her."

"Oh, fine," said the upstairs maid. "What do we do now? Run her in and plop her in Miz' Saravette's lap? And here comes old Dr. Trodden. He too old

to be doing this. He right 'trodden down' he'self. He can hardly get up them steps. Why don't they gits somebody young . . . ?"

"Shut up, girl," said Violet Mae. "First, it ain't none of our business, 'cept to tend to this baby Ginny right now, keep her quiet." As she bounced Ginny up and down on her shoulder, patting her back, "And get in there and finish up that dinner we supposed to be making! Slice up them carrots, hear? Miz' Saravette always loved candied carrots, her Mama's way of slipping vegetables to her, and finish peeling 'dose shwimps for Mr. Gavin's cocktail and put 'em on ice," she told the assistant cook, Lily White, glancing around the kitchen.

"Whoo! How can you talk about shrimp at a time like this?" shouted back her little assistant, Sudie.

"—an' go answer that front door and let the doctor in. And calm down. Don't screech at him like you did at me. Just take him to the sitting room, and be's pleasant."

Sudie hobbled up the hall, drying her hands, which were not wet, on her apron and adjusting

her cap before she reached the door and its still bing-bonging doorbell.

Saravette struggled to a sitting position to greet Dr. Trodden, but could not manage to stand up. Old Jack Trodden put his black bag down, pulled up a chair to her, patted her hand and immediately began to take her blood pressure. Gavin stood like a dead tree in the middle of the room and Genevieve leaned on a wing chair by the fireplace, hoping he would also take her blood pressure.

This child of hers never cried. Not since two years old. Not when she lost a tennis tournament. Not when she lost top place in the piano competition. Not when she was not invited to somebody's party growing up. Except she was always invited, even if she chose not to attend. She did not cry when she graduated from St. Catherine's, or when she left Juilliard after two years to marry. She did not weep on her wedding day. And here she was . . . who was this red-eyed waif sobbing on her sofa? Not her Saravette, not her rock, not her winner.

Neither Saravette nor Serena, not even the learned Doctors Chase Haughton Sr. and Jr. realized that Saravette was suffering from postpartum depression, first described by Hippocrates around 700 B.C., but not formally recognized by the medical community until the 18th and 19th centuries. Like legions of women before her, Saravette was instinctively hiding her symptoms, fearful and alone in her misery.

Chapter Eight

The Osprey's Influence

"Miz' Saravette, someone here to see you," called Daisy, her mother's new, very new maid, while Saravette was still visiting her parents in Richmond.

"Thank you, Daisy, I'll be right down."

Who in the world would just pop in to see me, without calling? She had not yet called her friends to say she was here, waiting a few days to have them for lunch or tea and show off the baby. She ran a comb through her hair and stepped down to the parlor, where Daisy had led the visitors.

"My goodness, Doc Haughton and Jim Horton,

too!" she said, seeing her father-in-law and the Haughton family minister.

She turned white and sat down fast. "What? What? Please, don't let it . . ."

"Chase is all right," said Doc Haughton, "but he did have an accident. We knew you would want to come home and be with him. We're here to give you a ride home." Reverend Horton sat beside her, took both her hands, and kissed her on the cheek.

"Serena told us not to call first, but I think maybe we should have. It couldn't have been worse than startling you like this. Here, sit back down," after she had jumped up.

"No, let me stand. What happened? Quick, tell me!"

"Chase had a fishing accident. Fell off a small boat, hurt his back, and is in the hospital in Greenville."

Angry and mystified, she demanded, "But why didn't he call me? Why all this to-do if he's all right? I could have had somebody drive me down there."

The men tried not to glance at one another, but failed. Of course, Saravette caught it.

"What is it? I know it's worse than you say. Tell me."

She stepped out the parlor door. "Mother," she called, toward the back of the house, "Come here, please."

In a moment, Daisy came to the door, looking nervous. She had obviously been listening at the back door.

"Your mother left out a while ago for the hairdresser, ma'am, back in an hour or so, I would guess. Shall I ring her up?"

With that, Saravette began shaking.

Her father-in-law and Reverend Horton then drove her straight from Richmond, Virginia, to the Greenville, North Carolina, hospital, then walked with her up to the third floor, down the hall to the left, to a room marked, "Dr. Chase Haughton, Jr. Do not disturb." She hesitated. They hesitated. A pretty red-headed nurse with freckles came up quietly from the nurses' station and said, "I know who you are, family, and I'll take you right in. Let me check him first and I'll come out and get you."

The nurse remained in Chase's room ever so long and returned. Closing the door, keeping her hand

on the knob, she looked quietly at each of the men, then at Saravette. "I'm so sorry. We might need to call his doctor, Dr. Knott, to handle this."

"Handle what?" Doc Haughton asked. "I'm a doctor and also his father. This is Rev. Horton, his minister. This is the patient's wife, Saravette. Can't he see us?"

"This is the problem," the nurse said quietly. "He's willing to see you, Doctor Haughton; you, Rev. Horton; but he says he cannot see you, Mrs. Haughton." Saravette stared speechless at the nurse. No one could look at Saravette. She was so shocked she couldn't cry. "Why not?" she whispered.

"Doctor Haughton says he cannot manage seeing you right now."

"Then, when?" Saravette breathed.

"I don't know," said the nurse, sorrowfully.

"Go ask him!" Saravette almost shouted. "Please," she added, softer.

"May I go in with you?" suggested Dr. Haughton.

The nurse hesitated, waved him on in behind her and closed the door. Saravette and Rev. Horton

stood alone outside the door of room number four, looking confusedly at each other, until she leaned against the wall and he reached for her, fearing she was about to slide down to the floor. Then, he led her to a chair up the hall, outside another patient's room, and sat her in it. She leaned forward on her lap and put her head in her hands.

"Dr. Knott, paging Dr. Knott. Please come to Room 4, Third Floor. Dr. Knott, Room 4, Third Floor."

Words failed both Saravette and Rev. Horton. They looked far down the hall, as if waiting for . . . What? Paralyzed with fear, confusion, they hadn't long to wait. A tall, dark-haired man—Dr. Knott, they presumed—rushed down the hall and swept by them, leaving a breeze in his wake. He spoke not a fare-thee-well to either of them, dashed straight into Room 4, and somebody closed the door behind him.

How long did they wait? Ten minutes? Twenty? Thirty? Presently, Dr. Knott emerged thoughtfully from Chase's room, closed the door, moved toward the paralyzed pair, placed his hand under Saravette's elbow, and guided them to a small waiting room

nearby. He sat her in the largest chair and pulled up a straight chair in front of her. He placed the back of the chair toward her, straddled it, his arms crossed on the back.

Remembering this moment clearly later, though it was not clear at that point, Saravette wondered if he had had a need to place the chair spokes between him and her to keep himself distracted, emotionally removed, in order to survive these career moments when he was invariably bound to make rational verbal logic on the spot, out of chaos, breakdown and disaster.

"All right," she started, "What is it? Is he all right? Nobody has told me anything except that he is alive. Why won't he see me? What happened? Please!" Finally, she did break down and cry, and cry, and cry. Saravette, the woman who had never cried in public before . . . until here . . . and now. No one tried to stop her.

After a few moments, Dr. Knott put his hand on her shoulder. "Look at me. Listen to me. I want you to understand. Whatever they told you, this is what happened. Best we understand it, your husband

was in his friend's boat down on the Roanoke River when an osprey flew down and landed on the side of a bucket of fish they had caught, stole one, flew away and startled the driver so that he jerked the tiller, throwing the boat sideways. Chase was thrown violently across the boat, landing on his back against the side, fell overboard and was almost washed down river, but they rescued him. The fall had broken his back, damaging the spinal cord so severely that he is paralyzed from the waist down."

"But," she looked straight at him, "he will live?"

"Yes, he will live. Right now, however, he is not really sure he wants to."

Her eyes grew wide. "No, you mean he . . . you're afraid to leave him alone? Is it that bad? Does he feel pain?"

"Hmmm. Yes, yes . . . and no. Yes, we do not dare leave him alone. Yes, it is bad. But, no, he feels no physical pain." Softly, "He wishes he did, feel pain."

Doc Haughton came out of Chase's room at the same moment as the nurse came over from the waiting room. Doc stood behind Saravette as she regarded the nurse.

"So. And when may I see him?" she asked.

Silence.

"You must understand, Mrs. Haughton."

"Please, call me Saravette."

"Of course. Try to understand. He is so devastated at his condition, he cannot face you or his little girl right now, not today, not tomorrow, we simply don't know when. He already feels he has died once. He thinks to look at you and the baby, he'll have to go through it all again."

"I'm sorry. I don't understand. He's a doctor. He can handle these things."

"Apparently not when it happens to him. This is beyond his experience. He's accustomed to helping others through loss. He cannot accept, it seems, being helpless himself."

"He's not helpless. He has me." She looked around at Doc Haughton. "He has us, his mother, the baby, friends, patients." Saravette was inspired. "Let–me–go–in–there–and–tell-him that if Franklin Roosevelt can run this country as President from a wheelchair, then certainly HE can mind a family

doctor's practice down here in Williamston. Let me just go right in there and tell him he can do it, too!"

The men stopped her.

They escorted her down the hall to the car, and drove her back to the Haughtons' house in Williamston.

Next day, she demanded to see her husband. No one could stop her. She called Ben-Olive to drive her to the hospital and marched up the stairs, into his room.

Directly she saw his eyes in their sockets, peering at her as if from the dark side of a prison cell. He threw back the covers to expose two legs, lying askew, as if unattached to the rest of his body, like dishrags carelessly thrown on a kitchen floor.

A voice she did not recognize asked, "Are you satisfied?"

Before she could catch her breath to speak, he was ringing for the nurse to lead her out of the room. The nurse must have been waiting just outside the door, as she stepped in immediately and gently led

Saravette out into the hall and down to the waiting room where Dr. Knott had told her Chase might not be able to see her for a while.

The nurse sat by her on the sofa and took her hand without saying a word. What could she say? Saravette knew she would never forget this horrible little room, the worn burgundy leather over-stuffed sofa and two monstrous chairs. Brass ashtrays on the end tables shaped like dull gold seashells; dusty old *Saturday Evening Post* magazines strewn about. She looked at the nurse, still holding her hand, who finally said, "I'm so sorry. I wish I could help you."

"I wish you could, too," Saravette murmured. "But nobody can. How long do you think it might take for him to take me and little Ginny back?"

"We don't know. We've never seen a case, a situation, like this before."

"Never?"

"I've only been nursing three years, but the doctors say they have not seen this one, either. They don't know how to advise you to keep trying to move him home with you."

Saravette suddenly realized that this, maybe-spoiled

man-child had always been used to being "on top," in control and—suddenly—was not. He could not deal with any of it.

Later that day, Saravette tried to talk with his friends who had been with him on the boat. She did not know who was the more miserable. They were deeply embarrassed, ashamed, and desperately wanted to make it up to him, to her.

Chase refused to see any of them for two weeks. Finally, the two men burst into his room. Chase's mother told Saravette how all three grown men hugged and cried and how he had asked her to leave the room for the rest of the boys' visit.

For the next three weeks, Saravette and baby Ginny stayed at the Haughtons' house, hoping she would pick up the phone and hear Chase say, "Sweetheart, I'm sorry for the way I treated you. I'm okay now. If you want to come here, we can manage this together. I want so much to see you. That was what our marriage vows were all about, right? For better or for worse, right?"

Chase never called. He did make one phone

call, however, to his attorney, Betty Ann Shannon's father, asking him to prepare divorce papers.

Of course, everybody in Richmond thought Saravette had left Chase, the young, handsome, small-town doctor who had been paralyzed in a boating accident. Her detractors declared how she just couldn't take it, the work of nursing a paralyzed man in a hick town, even with the good help his mother's servants afforded her and little Ginny.

Whenever they came home to stay with Grandmother Whittington in the heart of old Richmond, all the accoutrements were there for the baby: roses and lilacs in the garden, a play yard, a sand pile, and a playhouse for the little Virginia princess. Better yet, a gardener in the garden, a cook in the kitchen, a nurse in the nursery. Saravette could practice her piano, Mr. Elliot, all the day long, and she almost did . . . between bouts of crying herself to sleep, avoiding old friends and neighbors, and begging off going to church, shopping and the club. She was paler by the day.

Saravette never explained. How could she? *Who*

would believe that my husband, whom I adore, refused to let me see him, much less even try to tend him, help him dress, bathe him, help him exercise to build upper body strength, practice using his wheelchair, assist him at his office by receiving patients and relieving his nurse of some of the record-keeping? Wouldn't even let me bring baby Ginny in to cheer him up.

Saravette had pleaded with him over the phone to let her do all these things. He refused to listen. He held the phone without speaking, while she begged. After her first visit, even though he had left orders that she not be allowed to visit, she had tried again to see him, forcing herself into his hospital room.

She almost didn't recognize him, haggard, slack-jawed, grey-skinned, looking at least twenty years older. At first, she thought she was in the wrong room. Glaring at her, Chase had lost the playful light in his eyes. She recognized the cut of his jaw, the turn of his temple. This must be Chase, her husband. But, after regarding her with a cold stare, he waved her away, turned his head, and rang for the nurse to escort her out.

Through his father, he asked her to move out

of their house, which she did, and to ask him for a divorce, which she refused. But she did retreat, with Ginny, to her mother's house in Richmond. Next, Chase found a Norfolk lawyer to arrange some kind of "amicable" divorce, giving her custody of Ginny, but allowing their daughter to visit him at his mother's house three times a year.

Saravette rejected all of these extreme tactics, sure he was aiding in his own—and her—disaster. She was certain she could help Chase, help him get accustomed to his wheelchair and back to work. She was sure it could be done. Together, they could . . . .

But he refused to let her try. In effect, Chase had sent her packing, literally. His parents were also mystified, helpless. No one could believe he would do this to her. He was not himself. He would not discuss it with anybody, least of all Saravette.

Chase stared out the window in the summer, into the fire in the winter, refusing guests, pies, cakes, homemade muscadine wine, homemade booze, invitations to supper, rides to church. He closed their house on the farm outside town, moved in with

his parents, and let Boo and Ben-Olive take care of him. He took meals in his bedroom, and gradually allowed them to remove his football, baseball and tennis paraphernalia from the walls and give away his handmade boat paddle. His years growing up on the Roanoke River were over and done with, particularly that last day when the hungry osprey dove into the boat to grab a bass from the bucket. Chase wanted nothing to do with his past.

Saravette knew, when she returned to Richmond, that all of "Old Richmond" was whispering, then mumbling, and soon roaring its disapproval of her, or so it seemed. She could see the questions in their eyes, their cool inward manner, their looks, as she walked into a room and everyone grew quiet, eyebrows raised. Finally, one bossy old friend of her mother's came right out. She could not stand it a moment longer. She asked Saravette, in front of six people at a St. James Church ladies' circle meeting, "Now, Saravette, how was it you came to walk out on your husband after he had been in that accident on the river?"

Chapter Nine

The Garden Scene

"Mommy, Mommy, 'ook, 'ook. Idn't he coot? Can I eat it?" Ginny came running to her mother in the Whittingtons' rose garden.

"No, Baby! It's a worm! An earthworm. No. No. Put it back down on the ground! That is its home, Ginny. Put it back in the dirt!"

Ginny, a curious two-year-old, did not throw it down. It was pink and squirming, alive in her hand. She was hypnotized, not blinking, eyes enlarged, entranced by this live, magical pink creature. How could she know it was also treasured by her grandmother, wanting the earth in her garden to be blessed

by such useful, hard-working little laborers in her black soil, keeping it moist, aerated, and fertilized?

"Don't kill her," called Grandmother Genevieve, stepping briskly down the walk. "We need her." Ginny looked up at her grandmother as Genevieve removed the wiggling worm from her little fingers, walked over to a red rose bush, dug a hole near its roots and gingerly placed the little farmer down, whereupon it wriggled away into the soft, dark soil.

Both the young mother and her baby girl stared at the grandmother in awe of this short vignette in time that neither would forget: a picture of Grandmother saving, nursing, a worm . . . a worm! Grandmother Genevieve smiled broadly at them, just back from the beauty salon. Her white hair was perfectly shaped into old-fashioned finger waves, with one curl over her left eye. She wore an ankle-length lavender crepe dress with a linen-and-lace collar and a pearl necklace and earrings that were a wedding gift from Gavin. Her diamond wrist-watch had also been a gift from Gavin twenty years before. Genevieve never threw anything away—repair it, use it up, and wear it out.

Genevieve swept into the house and soon returned to the garden wearing her old faded gardening frock, straw hat, garden gloves soft from use, and worn rubber boots. She was in her element, the ground of her God. She had already requested of her Episcopal priest to use the old Baptist hymn, "In the Garden," at her funeral. Whenever Gavin spotted her in the garden, from the window of the house, he smiled, knowing his old bride was happy. He never joined her there, except for an occasional Dewar's scotch on the rocks in the cool of a summer evening. This was *her* world.

Knowing that golf was a game played by philosophers, Gavin had found his God on the golf course.

For some months, Saravette's old boyfriend "Bass" Baskerville had been calling again, having dinner with her family and escorting her to Junior League events. He was not unhappy with the turn of events that had brought Saravette back home. After all, he knew this was the way it should have been in the first place.

Chapter Ten

The Hotel Lobby

aving survived her second wedding six months before and a honeymoon on the Eastern shore at Bass's Aunt Jane's beach house, Saravette was trying to get back to normal, whatever "normal" was. She assumed "normal" was practicing piano for occasional concerts, adjusting to living in Bass's large, historic house, and figuring, most importantly, how to give darling daughter Ginny a happy life. With a new daddy, a new residence, and new grandparents added to her other two sets, the three-year-old had many names to learn.

One thing never changed: their special "story-and-talk" hour . . . well, thirty minutes. "Back to normal"

involved returning to Junior League activities, and so she did. At this moment, Saravette was leaving their monthly meeting, somewhat concerned about one of their programs to improve the reading skills of the colored children from across the tracks. All the members of the Children's Choir from Bishop James Johnson's Church of the Almighty Savior were in the reading program, so the Junior League ladies had invited them to come for a concert and lunch.

However, nobody but Saravette seemed to notice the rudeness of leading them off after the concert to eat their lunch crowded into the small room behind the kitchen.

Saravette asked the maître d', "Where are the children going?"

"Behind the kitchen, to have lunch, and a good one, too," she said proudly.

Saravette reminded her, "The last choral group we heard from St. Anne's School ate lunch in here, in the dining room, over by the windows."

"Yes?"

"Then why aren't these children who sang for

us today invited to eat in the dining room like the other singers?"

"Well, Ma'am," began the woman in the neat navy blue suit and white shirt. "It was not my decision, but, I guess, because they are from a Negro church . . . you can ask the business manager, if you like."

"The business manager! Ha! He'd just give me the 'business'."

"I don't know about that," the maître d' said, with a blank expression, "but he might ask you to tell the president of your organization, The Richmond Junior League." She looked helpless, a little desperate and ill at ease.

"Do they realize this is the year 1943, and we are at war with Nazi racists, yet you tell me these children cannot eat in our hotel's dining room? Their fathers are fighting and dying over there right now, dying to defend racial freedom . . . among other things?"

The woman in navy was clearly becoming very uncomfortable. "Yes," she said, quietly. "My husband is in the Army as we speak. And yours?" glancing at Saravette's wedding ring.

Blushing to her toes, Saravette mumbled, "My husband has flat feet, believe it or not, he really does, and a punctured eardrum from a diving accident." *Why do I feel the need to rattle on to this stranger? Obviously, it's time for me to close this conversation . . . why did I start it anyway?* she asked herself, but then said, "I hope your husband comes home soon." And she walked, embarrassed, toward the lobby.

The woman watched her go, laughing to herself. Her own husband was still stationed at Fort Bragg, North Carolina, training military dogs so they could go to war. Very specialized assignment. No one, not many, at any rate, could possibly take his place in the U.S. Army or any place else. He was the best at training war dogs.

As Saravette approached the revolving door, a short, chunky man with direct brown eyes stepped out from behind a potted palm, put his right hand up to his forehead as if tipping his hat to her though he wore no hat, and tried to hand her a manila folder. "Mrs. Baskerville, Mrs. Saravette Baskerville?"

"How did you know my name? Oh, this . . ," she

said, touching the nametag on her shoulder. "Yes, and you are?"

Ignoring her request, he insisted, staring directly at her without blinking, "I'm to hand you this packet to give to your husband."

"Why don't you give it to him yourself?"

"I've been told to tell you to give it to him."

"Told? By whom?"

"Well, by my sister."

"What's your name again? Where do you fit into this? Why are you here instead of your sister?"

Taken aback, he mumbled something about how he lived with his sister because he couldn't work as he had serious diabetes and she had to help support him because their parents lived on a farm in West Virginia and were not well . . . .

"Well, whoever you are, please tell your sister to give it, mail it, to him herself. He's away on business. His office address is in the phone book."

"She wants you to give it to him . . . with her blessing."

"Sorry, but this is silly. A strange man accosts me

in a hotel lobby to give a packet to my new husband and I don't even know what it is about. What *is* it about?" she asked, glancing at the large envelope still held out in his right hand.

"It's a bill for services rendered."

"Services rendered? What kind of services? Yard work?"

"Not that kind of services."

"Really, now. For some reason, I do not want to accept that envelope. You . . ."

"I don't blame you." His voice never changed timbre or volume. His eyes never blinked.

Beginning to feel trapped, she said, "I think I'd better call the police." As she began to glance around the hotel lobby, he said, "I think you'd better not."

"What did you say?"

"Nothing. There's nothing to say. You just take this packet, please, and give it to your husband whenever he comes home. And you two can discuss it."

Saravette sat down slowly in the nearest armchair. He sat in the one closest by her.

"Discuss what?"

"The information in the packet."

"It may not be any of my concern . . . or my business," Saravette insisted.

"You're right," he said. "It may not concern you, but my sister thinks you *will* be interested."

"Tell me again. What kind of services . . . rendered?"

"If I tell you, you may not give it to your husband."

"Maybe not. I don't even know if I will at all, 'til I know what kind of services were rendered."

"All I can say is, if you don't give it to him, somebody else will." He placed the large envelope between his right leg and the arm of the chair, leaned back and folded his hands across his stomach. "You obviously don't know that your present husband had asked another person, my sister, to marry him."

Shocked, she softly exclaimed, "You are quite right. I certainly did not know . . . . Did he offer her a ring?"

"Actually, he did. He gave her a ring . . . a ruby ring . . . a large ruby ring."

"Was it a *real* ruby ring?"

He clearly had never thought of that. After a pause, he said, "She assumed so. She trusted him. Are you suggesting she try to sell it?"

Stunned, needless to say, Saravette fidgeted with her cuff, gazed across the lobby toward the coffee shop, then out to the street. *Who are all those people? Who is Bass?* "I guess I can't quite take this in. When did he see her? When did this friendship start?" *Maybe he's lying.*

"When did it end? Is it over? He's been with me and my family . . . and daughter, almost every spare minute he's had . . . for the last year. How do I know this is the truth?"

"Mr. Baskerville began seeing my sister regularly about three years ago, up until a few months ago. Until she read of your wedding in the paper, she really felt he was going to marry her."

Saravette couldn't think of anything at all sensible to ask or say. Finally, she inquired slowly, "What led her to believe that they would marry?"

"He told her. She wore his ring. She planned her life around him. She told her friends at work about

him, and she told our family. She's a nurse at an old folks' home over in the next county. Oh, damn," he mumbled, "I've told you too much. We can't have you tracking her down. You understand. You do understand, don't you?"

"No, I probably do not understand anything. Nothing at all! So what is in that big envelope? A letter of congratulations?"

"Maybe." He eyed her again, sideways, deciding, and then he chose to tell her, "Listed in here, he will find every date, tryst, meeting, dinner, hotel, tourist camp, trips to the coast, the mountains, for which he never paid her anything, except for the ruby ring. And now . . . now, my sister is pregnant."

Silence. Saravette's knees turned to jelly, her stomach knotted, and she was very glad that she was already seated behind a potted palm.

Saravette wondered if she would ever speak again, to anybody. *Certainly not to this repulsive little fat man or to Bass, or to his parents, or to father, or mother, but still . . . he could be lying.*

So she did speak one more time. "How do I know

you're not lying . . . and your sister as well?"

He still did not blink. Cool cuss. "Uh, your husband has a birthmark under his right arm. You're welcome to open this up and compare the dates with those on your calendar, when he was away . . . when you were away."

"Why," she pressed him, "I mean, why didn't she, your sister, phone me if she wanted me to know?"

To say his answer startled Saravette was an understatement. "She thought, maybe, Ma'am—you might be willing to send her a little check by me, to help things along. She has to go to a doctor that she really can't afford, and she's not feeling well, you know, every morning. It's hard for her to get to work when she's not feeling so . . ."

"Stop! For God's sake, man. What do you take me for?" Saravette had never spoken to a person in this manner before. "While we're at it, Mr . . . . By the way, what is your name?"

Calmly, he replied, "Ma'am, it's best if I don't give you my name."

"Well, Mr . . . , tell me this if you can. Why aren't

you going instead to my husband to ask for money? Isn't he the cause of all this? Aren't you saying that he started the whole thing?"

"Oh, your husband already gives my sister some money to help with rent and groceries. He doesn't really know about me. I leave the nights he comes."

As his meaning became clear, Saravette almost threw up.

"Besides, he doesn't know she's expecting his baby. She's not ready to tell him." All this as if the nameless man were delivering tomorrow's mild weather report. On the contrary, Saravette felt a tornado whirling in her brain and she almost shouted, then glanced at the lobby and spoke carefully.

"You do know there's a name for this, don't you? Did I get it straight? You want me to stay quiet and hand out money to keep you quiet? Then, you go after him for more money? Every month? Every week? For her? For the baby? For you? For doctors and shots? For Lord knows what else? I certainly need to ask my husband . . . about it first. You do know you and your . . . sister or . . . is she your girlfriend? Your wife?" Her

mind was suddenly roiling with ideas of how couples could go about extracting money using . . .

"Blackmail. I can see you know what that is."

Actually, his face was a total blank. Expressing nothing, no embarrassment, no shock, no surprise. He still had not blinked.

Is he an actor? Does he have diabetes or not? Does he have a sister? Is all this just some con-man's idea of how to get some quick money from a woman coming out of her 'society' meeting? I've always suspected I'm naïve. I've been told that so many times.

Saravette thought again about contacting the police . . . but as they stared at each other . . . she knew suddenly, clearly knew, that every word he said was true. Furthermore, she also knew . . . that he knew . . . she knew.

A recent scene was racing through her brain, and some pieces began to fit. She remembered thinking one evening about two weeks ago, *It's six o'clock. Where is the man of the house . . . whose office is only a few blocks away?*

Bass had missed dinner almost every fourth night for several weeks. Sometimes he had offered an

excuse, sometimes not. If she attempted to inquire about his whereabouts, he had given her a curious smile and had slightly shaken his head. That night when she had asked where he had been while she and Ginny ate supper alone, he had turned on her.

"Don't I make you happy here? Most women would give an arm to live in this house. Two hundred years old, on the National Registry, on the best street in Richmond. You're a member of the finest club in the South . . . maybe in the country. Of course, this is not Martin County, but you certainly were not accepted in Williamston. You're playing the piano again. Everybody has quit talking about your divorce. I give you an allowance to travel, if you want to, with your mother or whomever. What else do you want?" He had said all this right up in her face.

She had been so shocked, she just mumbled something about . . . "Maybe you and I . . . we . . . could go on a trip together."

"And where would you and I go together? And carry Chase's daughter with us? Of course. Do you

really think you'd leave her? Oh, we could go to Italy for the opera or London for the symphony . . . isn't that your idea of 'travel'? For your baby to hear the best music? Or some such thing?"

Saravette had been startled, confused. "Where would you like to go? And without Ginny?"

"How about a romantic island in the Caribbean? Jamaica? Bermuda? No pianos, no babies. No concerts . . . just you and me?" He had stared her straight in the eyes. She remembered that she had cringed. He had felt it, seen it in her face. No mistaking.

"If you can be honest, Saravette, you must know that . . . you do not care one monkey's damn about . . . me. Why you married me, I do not know. This is a sham marriage and you know it. We both know it. I somehow in hell thought it could be different. Anybody in their right mind would know you still care about that clod doctor down there in the damn sticks. Where was my brain? God knows . . . How could I be so dumb?

And he had marched out, said he was going to the club to play cards. No supper at home that night,

either. He seemed to enjoy eating with the boys. Or with someone else? She had dismissed that thought then. After all, they were newly married. But now, she wondered . . . was all his ranting just a way to be with someone else?

Now, for some fool reason, she had to ask this annoying man behind the potted palm one more question.

"Is your sister pretty?"

Yes Ma'am. She is quite beautiful."

Backing away, she added, "Does she see him now?"

"Usually on Thursday nights."

Of course, dinner and cards at the club with the fellas. Boys' Night Out. And . . . boys will be boys— and I'm usually asleep when he comes in. Stupid, dumb, trusting me. Lying there, just snoozing away, like a silly idiot.

"One more question: how many other boyfriends does she have?"

Mr. No-Name looked away. No comment.

Saravette thought a moment, then told him, "You seem to know a lot about me and my husband.

You call me at home tomorrow and we'll discuss this further." She turned to go.

"But . . . I, I . . . need to know, Ma'am."

"Tomorrow. And do shut up. Please hand me the envelope and leave. Please." She arose from her chair and turned away, extending only her hand in his direction.

He handed her the envelope and scurried off.

Saravette stood in the hotel lobby behind the potted palm for a time. Then, she picked up the lobby phone by her chair.

"Operator, dial me . . . the Richmond residence of Mr. and Mrs. Richard Baskerville, please. Thank you." Saravette waited impatiently for the connection. "Lessie, do me two big favors, hear? Tell the cook to take next week off, with pay. I'll get back to her later . . . . No, no dinner tonight . . . . And you, pack up clothes for you, Ginny and me for a week. We are moving in with my mother this afternoon. I'll be there in thirty minutes to pick you up and go over to Mother's house. I'll call her from here and go by the bank to get cash for the cook . . . . And,

please . . . we want to be out of the house, leaving it locked before Mr. Baskerville comes home. All right? . . . Yes, thank you, dear."

She dialed again.

"Operator, one more favor, please? Would you dial me the Richmond residence of Mr. and Mrs. Gavin Whittington? Thank you." She snatched off her hat, threw it on the floor. Shaking her head, she grabbed at her hair as if to pull it out. Her mother answered and Saravette moaned wildly, throwing herself back down into the leather lobby chair, crying, "Ma-ma!"

Chapter Eleven

The Conversation

Two months later, still at her parents' house in Richmond where she intended to remain a while, Saravette sat in the garden with her mother and watched Ginny playing dolls in the dollhouse that Granddaddy had ordered for her. Her mother, of course, was asking questions.

"What did lawyer Gaines suggest about your request for an annulment? I'm sure he'll help you out best, as he's from an old family here, not close to us, but your fathers went to Episcopal High School together and he was in law school with your cousin, Will, at UVA, and . . ."

"Mother, please don't go on. You know all that 'good-ol'-boy' stuff doesn't mean a thing. Keep in mind, Bass was out with the 'ol' boys' club on Thursday night when this was all going on." Her mother still couldn't take it in.

"Saravette, you can't tell me all our friends' husbands run about every Thursday night after they eat and play cards downtown at the club. I still think they enjoy the good company and need to be away from the house and us women sometimes. It's healthy for them . . . so they don't feel like they're in jail. Give them a loose rein, I always say."

Her mother was embroidering initials onto a linen handkerchief and napkin corners for gifts. She'd always been good at embroidering monograms. Saravette couldn't sit still that long, except to play the piano. Her mother loved to sit and stitch and hum along off-key while her precious only child practiced scales, Bach, Beethoven, anything.

Today, Saravette did not care to continue their conversation.

"Mother, I'm sure most of the fellas go straight

home. 'Do not pass Go' and 'Do not collect one hundred dollars.'" Mama always smiled at any reference to the hours she and Saravette played Monopoly. Such happy, peaceful days. Those days without a former first husband in a wheelchair in Williamston, useless from the waist down, but remarried to that cute, red-haired nurse from the hospital. Those days without a new, philandering husband on the phone begging her to come back.

No lawyers in and out, searching for humiliating proof of infidelity as grounds for an annulment. No evading friends of all ages and opinions who seemed eager to take sides. Some were saying Saravette shouldn't be airing dirty laundry, embarrassing everyone. Others were saying, "So what? What's all the talk about? Really, what did Saravette expect from a good-looking, 'old-family' rich boy? Plenty of connections, money to spare, spoiled as a young prince?"

Was Saravette really as naïve as everyone had considered her to be? Pretty, smart, talented at the piano, respectful of her mama, but completely unaware of the real world? Even the women her age

who had been jealous of her growing up, despite being her friends and admiring her no end, carried such mixed feelings.

They did not know whether to feel sorry for her, or to say, "Serves her right," after leaving that sweet, crippled doctor-husband down in North Carolina. They had never believed, could never believe he had told her to leave . . . to go home and leave him alone.

Only a few friends called on Saravette and her mother at home. All, however, felt awkward and didn't know what to say because they were also friends of Bass and his family. Their husbands played golf and cards with Bass. Everybody in Richmond was put in a truly awkward position with this whole thing and wished Saravette had kept quiet.

Needless to say, Saravette hadn't told anyone other than her parents or her lawyer about the man behind the potted palm in the hotel lobby or about his wanting money for his "sister," who was purportedly expecting Bass's baby. Saravette had wanted to keep it low key for everyone's sake. Fortunately, the annulment had come through without much drama,

since Bass had been glad he didn't have to pay Saravette alimony. And Saravette had just wanted it over, as though it had never happened.

One Tuesday morning, after the venerable "Wednesday Morning Book Club," which more often met on Thursday mornings, except for an occasional Tuesday morning, according to the whim of the hostess, Saravette was walking out of the hostess's well-appointed library toward the even more lavish dining room for an exquisite luncheon. She briefly thought, *Maybe these members are more carefully selected for the brunch tables they spread than for the books they read. But, of course not. These are the best educated ladies in town. Perish the thought.* Her old friend, Mary Stewart Peacock, pulled her aside toward the morning room, touched her sweetly on the arm after chatting about this and that and got to what she really wanted to know.

"Saravette, what made you think Bass was running around?

Saravette looked at her concerned friend for a moment, two moments, before responding, "Mary

Stewart, I never said he was."

Mary Stewart stared at her a while, her mind whirling, and realized that Saravette had not publicly accused him.

But "Old Richmond" just knew.

She took Saravette's hand and they walked into brunch, invariably the best part of the meeting. The hostess today wanted to serve the freshest shrimp in her salad, which always came into the Richmond fish market on Tuesdays and Fridays. Her point being, "Never eat seafood on Monday." Today's hostess, Mrs. John Sterling, "Alice" to her friends, had never lifted a frying pan, but she could tell her listener every wise kitchen concept known to man, or rather, known to woman.

Her kitchen staff particularly appreciated her wisdom—as one can imagine.

Saravette's phone rang before breakfast the next morning and, to her eternal surprise, she recognized

the voice of her first husband, father of her precious Ginny.

"Saravette, I'll get to the point. What the devil is going on up there?"

The devil in her wanted to ask, "What business is it of yours?" But she said, "It's so nice of you to phone, Chase . . . what's on your mind?"

"I've already asked you, what's this all about?"

Chapter Twelve

A Phone Call, and More

Several weeks later, Saravette received a phone call from a gentleman whose name was vaguely familiar. Jonathan Donovan explained that he was an old friend of Chase's and that Chase had suggested he call her.

"I thought I had heard your name before," she said, slowly. "But how do you know Chase?" *Now, what is this about? I'm so weary of these eruptions from strangers out of the blue.*

His answer was interesting, although a little confusing at first. Jonathan was the youngest teacher at Virginia Commonwealth University Medical School

in Richmond when Chase was a student there. With similar medical interests and only a six-year age difference, they hit it off from the beginning. Jonathan and his wife, Patricia, often had Chase over for dinner when he was a student. Patricia had died young of cancer three years earlier and Jonathan had been on his own since. He had received a call recently from Chase, his friend and former student, who remembered that Jonathan loved classical music.

"Chase suggested I might call to ask you to join me for lunch or a concert and even mentioned that I would enjoy hearing you play piano. He said you play beautifully."

Saravette was stunned. She could not speak for a moment. Finally, she asked, "Your name again, sir?"

Kindly, he answered, "Jonathan Donovan, but my friends call me Jon."

Still taken aback, she heard herself say, "Well, Jon, are you still practicing medicine?"

"Yes, Ma'am, I sure am."

"If I may be curious, what is your field of practice?"

"Family medicine."

Her eyes lit up in spite of herself, even though he couldn't see her eyes.

"Oh, you mean you teach about treating babies, children, adolescents, and adults, as well as marriage and family health?"

He said, "Saravette, you described it as well as anyone I have ever heard."

She paused a moment after his compliment—she hardly knew what to say.

He interrupted her silence. "Saravette, may I accompany you to lunch this Saturday at 1:00 at Gerard's?"

She paused, wondering whether to accept. *This is so unexpected . . . what should I say?* "I've heard of Gerard's, but I've never been there."

"I'll be happy to pick you up."

"That's all right . . . I'll meet you there at 1:00." She wanted to be able to leave and catch a taxi home if this was not a pleasant, or interesting, occasion.

As she hung up, she wondered what had prompted Chase to suggest such a thing, and . . . what had caused her to agree to it.

Unknown to her, the truth was that Chase had not stopped caring for Saravette. He had later realized that what happened to him was not her fault and that he had hurt her. But at that time, he was so deeply depressed and utterly convinced he could not be the husband he longed to be, the active father he yearned to be, and the doctor he wanted to be. After his accident, he had painfully believed that he could be none of those things.

The miracle was that his hospital nurse, Mary Susan Staunton, with him daily, was able to draw him out of his depression and convince him that he could and would practice medicine again. During this time, she fell in love with him and was willing to be not only his nurse, but also his wife and his office nurse-manager. Her father was a doctor in Greenville, so she had a great deal of medical background in addition to her nurse's training.

A sense of duty was another reason Chase went back to practicing medicine. Because World War II was underway, his father had been called up to serve as a Navy doctor stationed in Norfolk. Chase knew

he should have been called instead, but realized his father had gone in his place, since he was not able to go for active military duty. Chase felt he needed to continue his father's medical practice, so he willed himself to develop the strength to take it over. That determination was the beginning of his recovery. Once he had found a form of happiness again, he wanted Saravette to have the same, both for her sake and for their daughter Ginny's.

Over the next few months, "Dr. Jon," as he was known throughout Richmond, continued to invite Saravette for various lunches, dinners and, most wonderfully, concerts of the Richmond Symphony. They were a handsome couple, the dark-haired, brown-eyed, slender Saravette and the tall, blonde, square-chinned Jonathan, with "twinkle wrinkles" on either side of his Irish blue eyes and a dimple when he smiled, and he did smile often.

One weekend, they even flew to New York City

for a Carnegie Hall concert featuring Vladimir Horowitz. While in New York, they had delightful dinners with some of his former medical school friends and some of her former Juilliard classmates. She could not remember having so much fun and feeling such happy energy in years. Their walks at dusk in Central Park during the gloaming, as the sun was lowering behind the trees, were some of the sweetest moments she had known. One special bench overlooking the lake, where she and Jon watched the swans, was somehow painted pure gold from the evening sun.

Back in Richmond, she felt confident enough to invite him for visits and dinners with her parents and, most importantly, with Ginny. On one of his visits, she fondly watched as Ginny ran to him, leaning on his knee and talking, nodding, smiling. Suddenly, Ginny ran from the room. *Where in heck is she going?* Saravette wondered. Ginny came back with her little violin case tucked under her arm. She walked close to Jonathan, opened the case, took out her violin, and began to play "Twinkle, Twinkle, Lit-

tle Star." Jonathan listened with intense delight and Saravette wondered if Chase would have expressed so much pleasure and encouragement in seeing Ginny's growing love of music.

Her family, friends and book club cohorts regarded Saravette with questions in their eyes. She knew they were thinking, "What's up now, Princess?" She refused to meet their eyes and they realized she was not about to share any details about her trips with Jon or their personal lives.

—m—

At dinner one evening in October of 1946, Jon asked Saravette what she thought of joining him on a New Year's Eve trip to Milan, Italy, for an opera that was taking place at the magnificent and romantic Teatro alla Scala. This impressive building had recently re-opened after being damaged during the war. Interestingly, the restoration had been partly funded by benefit concerts given by Arturo Toscanini, whom Saravette and Jon had first heard together at Carnegie Hall.

Saravette was beginning to realize that as wonderful as the man was whom she had thought was the love of her life—the doctor by the river in Martin County—this man, Jon, and she had much more in common, both in their interests and temperament. It was almost sinking in now that the Lord was keeping her in mind. That perhaps the Lord had used Chase to bring Jon into her life. It occurred to her that she was growing forever grateful for that.

What a dream trip! Italy! How romantic! She had never even envisioned such an experience, and had never thought, *I'm going to La Scala in Italy with a handsome, smart, kind, and musical man.* But as soon as she thought it, she knew she really wanted to go.

Even so, her first response was to laugh out loud. "You're not really serious, are you?"

"Saravette, you don't have to ask that question. You know I'm serious."

Then another thought struck her. "But Jon, what would my family think if I go to Europe alone with a man?" *Those Old Richmond gossips! This would certainly be grist for their mill, and wouldn't they have a*

grand time grinding up my reputation even further? Will this always be our future: just to be taking joint occasional trips together?

As she was thinking, he was already answering her spoken question. "Saravette, I already consider your family and Ginny to be part of my family. And I really think they trust me."

She looked him straight in the eyes, eyebrows lifted, and then realized that her family would be beyond thrilled. After all, they saw him as a mature, respected, successful professional who also shared her interest in music and played the violin himself. And, very importantly, he was genuinely fond of Ginny.

Then, bang, it struck her. *Of course, this is what Chase had in mind! He had known exactly what he was doing. He knew what my life needed. The pieces are all starting to come together.*

Needless to say, she accepted his invitation and began to think about making arrangements with her family to take care of Ginny over the New Year's holiday. They were, of course, overjoyed.

‒◦ New Year's Eve 1946 ◦‒

Saravette and Jon strolled along the streets of the recently war-ravaged city of Milan, on their way from the beautiful Piazza del Duomo, the central square of the city, to the opera house. They could feel the electricity and excitement of the city's rebirth, as well as its ancient roots.

The Gothic grandeur of the Duomo had been a glorious surprise to Saravette.

"It took six centuries to complete this massive cathedral, the fourth largest in the world," Jon explained. "Construction began in 1386 and was carried on through the centuries, and even now, it isn't quite finished. Napoleon brought it closest to completion when he ordered major work done in 1805, so he could properly be crowned King of Italy, making it a very historic building for many reasons."

Saravette was amazed at Jon's knowledge and his appreciation for the history and architecture of Milan, the great city of northern Italy.

Even after the impressive Duomo, when she first

caught sight of the illuminated 1778 La Scala opera house, she had to stop in her tracks, grab Jon's arm and whisper, "I cannot believe this building. It is stunning—radiant with light."

"Saravette, I thought you would admire it," he smiled. It struck her again that besides sharing a passion for classical music, they also shared a love for classical architecture.

She rattled on, "Jon, in the 1700's with no electric saws and lifts, how did they build such a structure?"

"Perhaps you and I both underestimate the genius of man," he murmured, looking up at the soaring roofline.

As they were ushered up to the box he had reserved, Saravette went to sit on his left, but he gently moved her to the other seat, on the right.

What difference does it make where I sit?

During one of the romantic arias, she learned why it made a difference . . . in the dark, she felt Jon lift her left hand, kiss it, and then she was aware of some activity concerning the third finger. She lifted it up to her face and saw a diamond there, sparkling

even in the mostly dark theater. She immediately looked at him, and, after one quick wink, he continued to follow the action on the stage, as if completely absorbed in the music and story of *La Bohème.*

She leaned forward, turning to see his face more clearly. Did she only imagine a slight shiver in his left dimple, a lift of his right eyebrow? Was that a question?

Sitting back, she took his right hand and whispered to him, "Well, . . . okay."

Saravette, now truly sure of her answer and diving in for good, squeezed three times—Yes, yes, yes! And added a smile in the dark for good measure.

About the Author

*L*ucia Powe earned her BFA in speech and drama at Wesleyan Conservatory in Macon, Georgia, and later attended UNC-Chapel Hill, Duke and East Carolina University for graduate work. Eastern North Carolinians remember her as "Miss Lucia" on the syndicated program, "Romper Room," produced in Greenville, N.C. Over

the years she has taught creative writing, speech, drama, music and art history at both college and high school levels.

Along with her first husband, Judge Elbert "Junie" Peel, of Williamston, Lucia reared four daughters (Lucia Claire Peel, Mimi Peel Roughton, Sydney Peel Woodside and Elizabeth Peel), one horse, and several dogs and cats. Widowed for ten years, she married another attorney, E.K. Powe, of Durham, the father of three daughters.

About the Artists

Emily Eve Weinstein

Emily Eve Weinstein has made her living as a full-time artist creating murals, portraits, fine art, and illustration, and also as a teacher over the past 40 years. Discovery Press has published her four published art gift books. At this writing she is working on the 25-year Handmade Book series. Weinstein has exhibited in the area and beyond. She is part of the Orange County Studio Tour each fall in Chapel Hill, N.C. More of her work is displayed at www.weinsteinart.com

Emily Eve Weinstein

About the Artists

Pamela Henry Pate

Pamela Henry Pate was born in and grew up in Atlanta, Georgia. After graduating from Wesleyan College, in Macon, Georgia, she began graduate studies in visual Art and Art History in Cortona, Italy. Returning to the U.S., she continued her graduate studies at Georgia State University, in Atlanta.

Pamela Pate completed her master's degree at the University of North Carolina at Chapel Hill. Pate is a National Board Certified Teacher and has taught visual Art and Art History to students from kindergarten to college. She lives in Chapel Hill with her husband and basset hound.

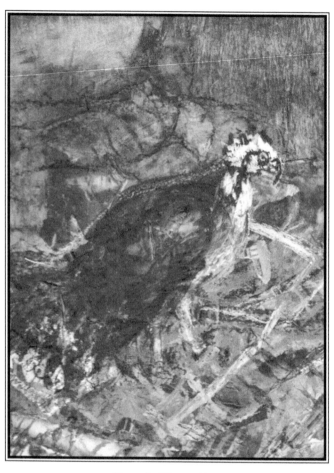

Pamela Henry Pate

About the Artists

Vita Jones

Reared and educated in the Pacific Northwest, Vita L. Jones has drawn and painted for nearly fifty-five years. After her Catholic education in Seattle, she attended Howard University, the University of Washington, The University of Cambridge, Parsons School of Design, and North Carolina State University. Formal discovery, intention and symbol are essential to this artist's aesthetic and to her work.

Vita has visited Europe, West Africa, and Central America, thus her purview is diverse, with particular inspiration from the genius of the Mayan people of San Lucas Toliman, Guatemala, on Lake Atitlan.

Vita wants her life to count for some civilizing act, a praise poem to a generous God, some intelligent response to the noise of convenience over substance. Her art has also been stretched and consecrated under the expert tutelage of Mary Whyte, international painter and human extraordinaire.

Her most pressing work is her children's book written and painted as promotion for KidZNotes' public-school violin program and slated for completion sometime during KidZNotes' fifth anniversary (2015-2016). Vita adds friend and fellow pilgrim, Lucia Peel Powe, co-founder of KidZNotes and producer of two novels, to her list of inspirations. Now she is most delighted to contribute to Lucia's second novel and privileged to aid and support the author's dream for the first.

Vita Jones

About the Artists

Myra Bowen

Myra Bowen is a Williamston, N.C., artist. While growing up in Lyman, S.C., she was an active Girl Scout who found a passion for nature and art in her many Scout activities. That led to a degree in biology and a career in teaching others about nature. In the 1980s and 90s she owned and managed a local arts and crafts store, then returned to teaching. Her love of the outdoors is reflected in her expressive works of art in acrylic, watercolor, pen and ink, or any mixture thereof.

Today she devotes her time to painting and sharing her love of painting with others. Several of her

works and prints are on display and available for sale on her website:

myrabowennaturallyinspiredart.wordpress.com.

"The aim of art is to represent not the outward appearance of things, but their inward significance."

~Aristotle

The greatest influences on Myra's work are her memories of places experienced while traveling and taking in the beauty of God's creation and human accomplishments. In her paintings, Myra shows how forms and functions within nature may seem simple at first, but are complex in ways that awe and delight. The ability of an artist to evoke an emotion within others from nothing more than a flat surface covered in pigments by an artist's brush in hand is one of her goals, and, indeed, several of her works have been awarded honors.

Myra Bowen

About the Artists

Christine Amory Long

Christine Long grew up in Lynchburg, Virginia, where as a young teenager she found solace in the creation of beautiful scenes at variance with the realities of her life. She completed her undergraduate education at Duke University, then joined the critical-care team in one of Duke Hospital's intensive-care units. In this emotionally charged, complex, and highly stressful environment, Christine developed the acute observational skills, the attention to detail, and the desire for excellence that became the foundation of her artwork.

In 1995 she began a decade-long study with

master artist Frank Covino in the classical academic techniques of the Renaissance. Since 2007 she has pursued a career in art, winning a number of awards in juried shows and attracting patrons from North Carolina, Virginia, Florida, and Maryland. She's a member of the Durham Art Guild, the Nasher Museum of Art, and the North Carolina Museum of Art. Her work may be viewed in her studio, the Millenaissance Studio at Golden Belt, in Durham, North Carolina. Christine also restores 19th and 20th century oil paintings.

Her oil paintings show a world serene and beautiful, yet tinged with the awareness that beauty is fleeting and should be appreciated fully in the moment. The work evokes a dynamic tension between light and dark, near and far, life and death, achievement and possibility. Moments of quiet repose yet also contemplative isolation are lovely on the surface, but a deeper study hints at metaphorical allusions to man's relationship to himself, to the natural world, and to humankind.

ONLINE GALLERY

The paintings of Christine Long may be viewed online at
www.flickr.com/photos/21562615@N04 or by going to
www.flickr.com and doing a people search for paintercal.

Christine Amory Long

About the Artists

Elaine O'Neil

Textile artist Elaine O'Neil grew up in rural Maine, the great-granddaughter of a lighthouse keeper, granddaughter of a farmer, and daughter of an ardent seamstress.

She received a degree in textile design from the Philadelphia College of Textiles and Science, and has shown her work in galleries up and down the East Coast as well as in the mountains of North Carolina.

Elaine regularly does commissions and has created textile collages for clients in Russia, England, Greece, Italy, and France, as well as in many states in the U.S.

Her work is also in the collections of many colleges, businesses, and hospitals, on the cover of several books and publications, and she has illustrated two children's books.

Elaine says of her work, "My artistic process begins with the simple, pure memories of my child-hood. I conjure up those good times in whimsy and color, stitching them together with a sense of humor and delight. My process begins with a simple sketch. Then through snips and cuts, my scissors, like a painter's brush, slowly reveals the image. Layer upon layer of fabric, stitched into place using a variety of colors and textures, brings the piece to life. In each piece, my hope is to evoke the pleasure and delight of childhood, when life is simple, sweet, and full of endless possibilities.

"This will be the fifth year I have created my Luv This Place® North Carolina art calendar featuring the places and culture of North Carolina. A percentage of the proceeds is shared with the N.C. Cancer Hospital. I have illustrated a few children's books—most recently, *Goodnight Carolina*, and have been fortunate to have my work featured on the cover of other books and many magazines."

Elaine O'Neil

Special Thanks to

Bland Simpson

Author of *Little Rivers & Waterway Tales*, *The Coasts of Carolina* and *Inner Islands*. Long-time pianist for Red Clay Ramblers, and the Tony award-winning string band Director of Creative Writing at UNC-CH.

CPSIA information can be obtained at www.ICGtesting.com
Printed in the USA
BVOW11s0857310116

434539BV00011B/5/P